CHI CHAVANU ÀSE

Journey To Ghana and Other Stories

First published by Vital Narrative Press 2020

First edition

Editing by Gregory Hedgepeth
Illustration by MALICIOUZ

This book was professionally typeset on Reedsy.
Find out more at reedsy.com

To my mother, Kamili Siglowide. Thank you for choosing me and allowing me to choose you. Thank you for introducing me to our favorite genre: science fiction.

Contents

This author supports:
- Carefree Black women and girls
- Black Lives Matter
- Trans folk
- The Queer community
- Sex workers
- Gender equality
- Melanated immigrants
- And every marginalized group that does not cause harm

Trigger/content warning:
- murder
- rape
- sexual assault
- sexual assault of a child
- graphic details of violence

I

Part One

"Sometimes it hurts to breathe. Sometimes you have to remind yourself to breathe. Here is your reminder to breathe."

The Healer (Pre-apocalypse)

The white witches were at it again with their foolery. They acted a fool so much, I never knew which threat to take seriously. Nanabaa told me to take all threats seriously, but I didn't have the patience or the time. Today while on my daily walk, this goof dressed in all black kept mean-mugging. She had all the aesthetics, per usual. Her skin was paper white, her thin lips were darkened with black matte lipstick, and she had the type of face you wouldn't look twice at.

"A healer, your precious Blessed will need you!" she hissed. She started cackling. "And so will those filthy regs!" *Deep breath in, deep breath out.* I got threats from white witches at least once a week. Whether at the grocery store with my wife, taking the trash out, or leaving my job, white witches were constantly attempting to hex me. I was a target because I was not just a healer, but a Black healer. I was *Blessed* with certain abilities to heal others like me, those with magic or some type of essence in their bloodline. I was unable to heal "Regs" or regular humans, so during the day I worked with them as a therapist. At night is when I physically heal the *Blessed*.

My blackness intimidated white witches fueled by racism, leaving me open to their harassment on a weekly if not daily basis. It was exhausting. It's interesting—when you think of racism and prejudice, you don't think of it amongst the Blessed. We're all used to racism amongst the regs, but racism amongst the Blessed seemed so primitive.

Back to this attention-seeking-cauldron of doom. The white witches were planning something. The witch had marked every other tree and bush on the walking trail, and I couldn't help but feel uneasy. This felt different. I wasn't scared, because *Blessed* were not allowed to harm a healer, but for some reason, her threat was weighing more heavily than any other threat before. I don't know why, but I felt like I was supposed to be paying close attention to her actions. I turned around, and of course she had already disappeared. *Cheap parlor trick ass!* But now I needed to figure out what she was doing. Why mark every other tree, and every other bush? She had even marked a tree with a Sankofa symbol. This was especially dangerous because the Sankofa symbol meant that this territory belonged to an especially powerful witch. She was asking for an ass whooping. What would make her sign her own death certificate? Where did this sudden burst of confidence come from?

I needed to locate Nanabaa, but she wasn't an easy person to find. When she wasn't doing healing work, she was off somewhere making money. Either way, she didn't like being disturbed and preferred to find you before you found her. I knew someone who could find her easily though. I just hoped he was in his usual spot.

Downtown Sacramento had a large homeless population, so this wouldn't be an easy task. Lucky for me, only one of them was the dopest rapper alive. If I knew Pulse like I thought I did, he was somewhere in the middle of a freestyle battle. Pulse wore sunglasses and walked with one of those sticks for the blind. No one knew for sure if he was blind, but we treated him as such.

Stepping out of my car, I immediately felt the change in the air. Nobody appreciated outsiders. At the steps of the capital, someone had set up a tent for the night. I peeked in and didn't see Pulse.

"Looking for someone?" a leathery old woman asked in a gravelly voice.

"No" I replied and quickly kept moving. *Where the hell was he?* I needed him to find Nanabaa. It was getting darker, and as I waded through those that society disregarded most, I could feel my anxiety building. Half these folks were *Blessed* and hurting, and I didn't have the time to heal them. The hostile stares were getting more intense, so I decided to turn around and look for him in the morning. Then I heard a familiar voice:

"Pretty brown girls
  Like diamonds and pearls
  But pretty will surely fade
  What's a girl like you doing down in the grunge?
  You should fa-sholey stick to days"

Pulse had found me and was speaking the only language he knew: rhymes. I didn't have the patience for it, but I knew what I had to do.

"Not too pretty for this convo
  So, come close and please humor me
  I came to you for some info
  What will it take for you to help me?"

"My belly been empty for two or three days
  You came through looking like a snack

5

I can guarantee a passage that's safe,
But my goons eat the rich that's a fact"

"Don't ever forget I was raised in the Heights
I went to school in Oak Park
But let me call up the pizza guy right now
They might not come out if it's too dark"

I ordered about fifteen boxes of pizza, and finally, Pulse agreed to sit down with me. "I need to locate Nanabaa," I explained. "It's an emergency." Pulse was a tracker who could track anyone and any being on earth. He was so skilled that he didn't even need a personal item like most trackers. He just needed to visualize the person. Most times, people didn't know that they were being located, but Nanabaa could always tell—she had so many talents.

"Now you know Nanabaa ain't wit no tracking sh—"

"Pulse, it's an emergency." He hesitated, but reluctantly started the process. His hands started to move up until they were almost in front of his face. He started gently stroking the air, and it was almost as if he was sculpting Nanabaa's face. It was like watching an artist create an exquisite piece of work. Watching him in awe, I couldn't help wonder how life might have ended up differently for him. One moment, he was signed to the top recording label, and the next, he was sleeping on a bench in downtown Sacramento.

"Don't do that thing
Where sorrows fill your brain
Don't feel sorry for me
Just let me show you my swang"

6

He had located Nanabaa. I hugged him fiercely and walked quickly to my car. It was after dark and I knew the *Blessed* would need me. I needed a night off or at least a few hours. Despite the darkness, it was only seven p.m., and I had work to do.

I knew that Nanabaa was going to be pissed that I interrupted whatever she was doing. Sometimes, she was interdimensional, which took her longer to come back from. I always found it interesting when she was interdimensional, because she often encountered herself in a different time period or dimension, which I had always heard was a taboo. However, Nanabaa insisted that she enjoyed spending time with herself in any given dimension.

I decided to run to the store and get some of her most favorite sacred items: jalapeño cheddar cheese pops, brown liquor and caramel candy. Luckily, there was a liquor store nearby that sold all three. After locating each item, I stood in line and waited my turn. The dude at the counter was getting agitated with the cashier. I couldn't hear everything going on, but I could see the cashier had a fearful look about him. The customer shouted in Russian that he wasn't paying for shit. Healers could understand all languages, one of the perks of such an exhausting job.

Suddenly, the agitated customer switched to a language that I shouldn't have been hearing at 7:15 PM in the middle of a convenience store. I heard Nwansena, which could only mean one thing. "You're all gonna die soon!" he yelled. "Once the witches unleash my brothers and sisters, we will all be free!" I quickly touched the human in front of me on the shoulder and she fainted into my arms.

In fluent Nwansena, I told the man he was violating code 214.3 by speaking Nwansena in public, and that he needed to leave the premises. To my horror, the man started to shed his human form in front of me. I could see that this was about to get ugly. In English, I screamed at the cashier's wife to turn off the lights and hide. Most monsters could see perfectly in the dark, but humans could not. I needed some cover to save the human customer and the cashier.

I dragged the human outside to her car. After grabbing her keys, I finally got her into the seat. I gently tapped her on the shoulder to wake her. She woke up confused and I told her about a place that served excellent soup. Whenever I had to wake someone suddenly, I always tried to have a backstory ready. Still visibly confused, she put on her seatbelt and presumably drove somewhere with incredible soup.

I ran back into the dark store and heard Kankabi. *Two members of the Blessed in one space?* I shouted in Kankabi for the lights to be turned back on. The lights came back on, and I saw two Kankabis' and one Nwansena. The Kankabis' resembled human size millipedes, while the Nwansena resembled a human size house fly. What the hell was going on? In one voice, I stated the laws and violations of shedding human form in a public or human setting.

The Kankabi understood, but felt they were in danger and had to defend themselves. The Nwansena, who had been fluttering back and forth, landed on the linoleum. "Humans have had the space for long enough. It is not fair that I have to wear my human form to make them feel comfortable. It's not fair that my true form is unacceptable, but my human form is. My human form sucks and I refuse to transform back!"

Listening to the Nwansena lament, I couldn't help but feel that he was making valid points. The *Blessed* shouldn't have to make themselves palatable for the human gaze, but they do. I gently explained to him what the rules were and the cost of violating

8

the rules. I also let him know that if he did not transition back to his human form, he would get the attention of the Radar, police for the *Blessed*. Even through his Nwansena eyes, I could see the fear around the Radar. He immediately started to transform back. His transforming helped the Kankabi feel comfortable enough to transform back to their human form. Naked, the female Kankabi wanted to know what was next? I hated to tell them I had to report them all, but I did. I did not want any run-ins with the Radar, and I could not risk anything because of them.

"They will probably just fine you and your husband. I am sure it won't be anything too terrible." I honestly wasn't sure.

Pulling into my driveway, I felt depleted. The entire day seemed like a blur, and the clock only read 8:21. As I got out of the car, dizziness hit me. Grabbing the car door to keep balanced, I knew exactly what was wrong. The world was ending.

I hated when my wife forgot to leave the porch light on. After entering the house, I fumbled around in the dark to find the light switch and was greeted by a familiar voice. "Lee still forgets to turn the light on for you? Figures." After finally finding the switch, I flipped it upward and light flooded my living room revealing a stunning Nanabaa. Standing at least six feet with her stripper heels on, an Ankara print Kimono, and black silk lingerie, I could tell that Pulse must have interrupted her on a date. *Look at my grandma out here being fast!* I'm glad she was dating though. She had given up a lot to raise me, and dating had never been her priority. I hadn't even sent a signal yet; she came just based off Pulse tracking her.

"If you had a spouse, then you would know that they forget everything," I responded.

"Now Brit, is that any way to talk to your most favorite

grandmother?" she replied. As we embraced, we bantered back and forth some more, talking mess to each other and throwing shade in the most loving way. I needed this. I needed all of this.

"Nanabaa, I—"

Before I could finish, she interrupted and demanded a hot-toddy. "Whatever you feel is urgent, I can assure you I will be at my best after a warm drink."

Lemon, brown liquor, hot water, honey, and a tea bag was her concoction of choice. Handing her the cup, I could feel myself relaxing. She always did this. I had always felt that she gave off relaxing energy as part of her abilities, but she assured me it wasn't the case. I almost didn't feel like talking about anything. The witch, the Nwansena, and the impending doom that hung over the city like a cloud all seemed insignificant. I just wanted to sleep.

I got up from the loveseat and found myself with my head on Nanabaa's lap. She scratched my scalp and sang a traditional song about a little girl in Ghana who gets eaten by a crocodile. It probably wasn't the best song, but hearing Nanabaa's beautiful voice made it worth it. "Now, there is nothing you can do except wait for this storm," she said. "Then after the storm is over, do your job."

The next morning, I was ready to strategize and prepare for whatever was coming. I called out of work in anticipation of us utilizing my house to come up with a game plan. I heated up some leftover jollof rice and chicken. I waited until noon to knock on the guest room door where Nanabaa was sleeping. I hadn't even knocked yet when Nanabaa emerged. She looked like she hadn't even slept, but there were no bags under her eyes or saggy skin—just a beautiful mahogany goddess, blessing me with her presence.

"Nanabaa! Can we take a moment to talk about the world ending?"

She poured hot water into her mug and searched the cupboard for a tea bag. "You look so beautiful in bright colors. When you were a child, I loved to dress you up in beautiful fluffy dresses." I tried not to roll my eyes, but she was already getting on my nerves. Nanabaa had a way of not really answering a question. Her mind sometimes was still in another dimension... or decade.

"Nanabaa, I think we should prepare for what is coming."

She smiled at me, amused. "Let's take a walk."

I liked the satisfying crunch of stepping on dried-up leaves, but since they had just started falling off the trees, there was no sound when I walked on them. Nanabaa was wrapped in a fur coat, even though it was seventy degrees outside. She did the most. We walked in silence for over 15 minutes, and it was killing me. I decided to walk to the end of our cul-de-sac, to check the mail. One of my neighbors was also checking his mail. "Hey Brent. How is everything going?"

Brent had been looking down at his mail and looked up to say hello. He squinted. He looked at Nanabaa, then looked at me. "You got a visitor? How long is *he* staying?"

I felt that familiar sting. "*She* is wearing a full face of makeup, a fur coat, and stiletto boots. Why the hell would you misgender her as a male? My grandmother is a woman."

Brent's goofy face turned red. "Well, *it* looks like a man with lipstick."

Now, my hood-button was fully activated. "Listen here, you dried up streak of bird shit! My grandma—" Nanabaa, who had been smoking a long cigarette, stopped me. She grabbed me and pulled me towards my house. I was fuming, but she didn't seem to care. "Why aren't you as mad as me?"

She smiled and inhaled some smoke. "Sweetheart, the same man that goes out of his way to misgender me, is the same man who will inquire about me spending the night. I do not like it, but he does not deserve my energy or yours. The world is ending—and Brent will be dead before sundown."

Nanabaa wasn't being forthcoming. The whole walk home, she did her best to not answer any questions. I could not take it anymore. I walked in front of her blocking her path. "Nanabaa. What do you know about the world ending?" Nanabaa stood real still and looked up at the trees.

"Do you remember your eighth birthday?" I sighed. How could I forget? My parents died two weeks later. "I had bought you a gorgeous fluffy pink dress. We were throwing you a surprise birthday, and you had somehow found out. The days leading up to the party, you stressed about people finding out about you knowing about the *surprise* part. The day of, you threw up and all the guests had to leave. You felt bad knowing about your surprise birthday party, and felt you ruined everything."

I sat on the end of the sidewalk and waited for whatever I was supposed to gain from the story. "Nanabaa, I'm not understanding the lesson from this."

She sat down beside me on the curb. "You do your best work, when you don't know everything."

We made it back to the house to find my front door wide open. *Had Lee come home early from work? No. She would have texted me.* Cautiously, I peered into my living room. A water *Blessed* was sitting on my couch, bleeding. His arm was completely severed and laying in his lap. He was soaking wet and had gills around his neck. I assumed he lived in the pond behind my house. "What happened? Who did this to you?" It appeared that he was stuck in mid-transformation, between his *Blessed* and human form.

12

His lips were turning blue, and due to shock, he couldn't even speak. After further examining his arm, I could see that it had actually been bitten off. *What would have been able to bite his arm clean off?* I got to work healing his arm and looked up at Nanabaa, who was comfortably seated on the other couch.

With the teacup to her lips, she whispered three simple words: "So it begins."

II

Part Two

*"Who would you become to continuing existing?
What does that monster look like? Certainly, that
monster wears no mask."*

Belly (Pre-apocalypse)

I reached for my headache medicine. I could tell that today was going to be one of those days. I searched for the water bottle that I kept beside my bed just as our bedroom door burst open and the twins ran in.

"Deronn said that we can only open the blueberry pack of waffles, but I want to open the regular kind. You said we can only open one kind and I do not think it is fair that we always choose his because he was born two minutes before me." Imani's face was twisted in her worrisome expression that was more adorable than anything else. I knew this was a serious concern, but I was far too exhausted to take it seriously. Being part of a major research team made my schedule super hectic. My husband was the more reliable parent with set hours for his shop.

Despite my exhaustion, I knew this was a defining moment for both children. "Whoever chose last time, it's the other person turn to pick," I explained. Imani squealed with delight and Deronn shook his head as they both ran out the door.

The door to our master bathroom creaked open, and my husband peeked his head out. "Well played, Mom."

"I am convinced that you stayed in the bathroom the entire time, so you wouldn't have to intervene."

I smiled at my beautiful husband as he exited the bathroom.

"I would never ever get in the way of two eight-year olds and their choice in waffles—I care about my safety." I threw a pillow at him as he smiled and shrugged.

My team had decided to give us a much-needed self-care weekend. We had been going so hard for months, we deserved it. The kids wanted to go to the Children's Museum in San Francisco and the weather was supposed to be sunny. As long as we were on the road by ten, we would make it to San Francisco by noon. I loved the Bay Area. I wouldn't mind living there if it wasn't so expensive. I didn't really feel like driving, but I chose to drive down there since we had agreed that I had to drive at least one way.

I tried to focus on the road, my husband, and the kids, but I kept thinking about my research. I was the second lead for a project that focused on trauma and its impact on the brain. I had a PhD in neuroscience and an MS in neuropsychology, so I was ideal for the project. At the moment, we were examining the brains of the deceased who had suffered some type of severe trauma while they were alive. We were comparing samples to those who were still alive, but had suffered the same trauma. It was exhausting work, and I was currently waiting on results from a test sample.

"Nzinga, you didn't hear a word I just said, huh?" I knew he was annoyed at me because he called me by my name instead of "babe." I felt bad. This was not the time to be thinking about a test sample. This was the time to be enjoying the present.

"Forgive me, can you repeat it?" He shook his head and looked out the window. I needed to do better. My husband had taken on so many roles since I had started the research project. With me also being on call at the hospital, I was barely home, so I appreciated our dynamic. I knew being the owner of an auto repair shop and a full-time parent was no easy task. He originally went to college for engineering, but was making so much money doing freelance mechanic work, he dropped out and went to a trade school. With everything he did for all of us, the least I could do was listen to him. I needed to make a greater effort to be present in the moment. He deserved it. We deserved it.

"Mommy, the bridge is coming up!" Deronn announced excitedly. This was undoubtedly the twins' favorite part and my most dreaded. *It was just a freaking bridge! How could someone who had performed brain surgery be terrified of bridges?* My husband instinctively read my mind and put a reassuring hand over mine. He was annoyed I hadn't caught his entire story, but he still loved me. "Two more miles, and we will be on the bridge!"

All I had to do was get over the bridge and it was smooth sailing. I could feel myself holding my breath, but I kept telling myself it was going to be a piece of cake to calm my nerves. *Focus on the moment and soon we will be enjoying a day in the bay!*

But before we could make it halfway across, the bridge began to shake and the car in front of us slammed on its brakes so abruptly, I had to come to a complete stop, causing the car behind me to rear end us.

I cursed. "Is everyone ok?" Turning around, I ran my hand over the twins to make sure there were no cuts or breaks. They were terrified, but they appeared to be fine. Turning back to the front, I couldn't even comprehend what I was seeing.

Ahead of us, the bridge had several off-white metal pieces that were breaking apart the cars—it almost looked like the bridge was eating them. *What type of machinery was that and how did it malfunction?* I was so confused, I mumbled the thoughts out loud to my husband.

"I don't think that's the bridge," he responded with a fearful look.

I didn't understand. *What else could be breaking the cars?* The next few minutes were something out of a movie.

Screaming.

Moving cars.

Bridge eating cars.

Bridge eating us.

Darkness.

* * *

My head throbbed. I attempted to open my eyes all the way, but my head hurt. It was dark outside. My arm. Something was wrong with my arm. It hurt hella bad. *Was it nighttime? Did I hurt my arm in my sleep? I felt around for anything familiar. My nightstand. Where was my nightstand? Was that a seatbelt? What the hell was going on? Why would I be feeling my seatbelt, if I were in bed? Am I in the car?* I told myself that if I could find my phone, I would be able to figure out what was going on. I felt around in the dark, but couldn't find it.

Using my left hand, I unbuckled my seatbelt. My right arm was throbbing. I stretched forward feeling for anything on the floor. *Where was my phone?* I needed some light. It took me over five minutes before I remembered that I could just use the lights inside the car. I pushed the one nearest to me and screamed.

My husband had been here with me in the darkness the entire time, slouched over. There was blood on his face. *If he's here, are the kids here too?* I was terrified to look behind me, but eventually I turned and saw that both were in the backseat. Their eyes were closed, and I was scared that when I went to feel for a pulse, they would be dead. Ignoring my arm pain, I turned my full body around and checked to see if they were alive; I breathed a sigh of relief when I realized that they were.

I pulled some ice out from the chest and rubbed both of their foreheads gently with it, while also grabbing some for my arm. They groaned and slowly started to wake up. They must have fainted. I came back to the front and checked my husband. I was scared he was dead. I checked for his pulse. He was alive, but still unconscious. I moved his head into the proper resting position and waited. I hadn't even thought about what was going on outside of the car until I saw a faint light right outside my window. *Is that another car? Why would another car be so close? Maybe we were we in traffic and the entire city lost power. But why couldn't I see the moon? Stars? Streetlights? Anything?* Everything was infinitely black.

"Mommy, did the monster kill us?" Deronn asked. *Monster?* I turned around to assure my son that there was no monster, and that we must have gotten into some type of accident. "No, mommy. The monster ate all the cars in front of us, and then it ate us. It had rows of teeth." We must have seen a shark. I needed a moment to think. *Did we end up going to the San Francisco aquarium on the pier instead of the museum? Is that where he saw the shark?* I was having a hard time putting the pieces together, and everything on my body was beginning to hurt. More lights started coming on outside of the car. We were surrounded. I couldn't make sense of anything. The car next to me shined their phone light into ours.

I started to roll down my window when the person holding the light banged on the glass. "Don't open it!" they yelled with a muffled scream.

Our cars were pressed together so closely, we could literally touch each other. Holding up a rather large phone, I noticed they had typed something. "Do you know what happened?" I shook my head no. I looked around for my phone and found my husband's instead.

I grabbed it and typed back. "Do you?"

He responded quickly. "I think we were swallowed by a whale."

Using the flashlight on the phone, I turned off the light inside the car and shined it through the windshield. We had a small parking lot full of cars surrounding us. I typed that there was no way we were in a whale and held up the phone. His eyes widened and he nodded his head in agreement. I was scared, and my husband was still out. I waited and waited some more. The twins fell back asleep. I saw lights starting to come on inside the cars all around us. It looked like they went back almost a mile. I looked up and saw the guy from the other car attempting to open his door.

I flashed the light on my phone. "Not yet," I typed.

* * *

At some point, I fell asleep and was awakened by a commotion. I wasn't sure how long we had been in the dark, but I could hear distant screams and our car began to move. I flashed my light and looked over at the man from the other car, who looked just as confused as me. Suddenly, our car lurched forward. *Oh my God, what is going on? And what is that smell?*

To my right, I heard my husband make a noise. "My head," he moaned. I quickly jumped into action and held his head in a way that was supportive of his neck. As he opened his eyes, I could

22

see the confusion across his face and quickly caught him up to date. He turned around to check on the children. I didn't want him to wake them, but he said he needed to hear their voices.

"Are we inside the monster?" Imani asked. I looked at her and said that was impossible.

My husband remained annoyingly quiet like he always did when assessing something. "We may... or may not... have been swallowed," he said simply.

I decided to take a moment. "I have assessed this entire situation while you were out. Seeing how many cars are in front of us, it's impossible for us to have been swallowed. Deronn said he saw rows of teeth like a shark, and there is not one shark I can think of that could swallow over a mile's worth of vehicles, not even a Megalodon. At a moment like this, maybe we should be careful in terms of indulging the twins' imagination."

I could tell immediately that this was about to start an argument. Three months earlier, we had gotten into a huge argument about the twins that really tested our marriage. It was the worst thing we had ever gone through. The three of them were at a stop light and the kids swore they saw a woman turn into another woman. My husband didn't see anything, but it turned into a huge ridiculous mess, because the twins were convinced. Eventually, he caved and agreed that they actually saw the transformation, and now, we are all in therapy.

"I saw us get swallowed," he said. "Don't you remember when you asked why the bridge was eating the cars ahead of us? Not long after that, you passed out—but I saw everything..."

This was too much. "Ok, for the sake of argument, let's say we were swallowed by something. It would have to be massive and I cannot think of one animal known to man that can swallow hundreds of cars."

23

Deronn finally spoke up. "Just because it does not make sense to you, doesn't mean it isn't real." I sat back and remained quiet. I needed a moment to think.

* * *

I fell asleep again. *Why am I so sleepy?* I felt the car moving again, and this time the screams were not so distant. My phone. I had finally found it. I tried to call 911, my mother, his mother, hell, even the Chinese food place by our house. Nothing. Absolutely no service. It was like we were inside a brick building. Frustrated, I checked on everyone. Everyone was sleeping, but everyone was breathing. I decided to check on our neighbor. I shined my phone into his car and saw him slowly stir. He had been sleeping as well. I mouthed if he was okay and he nodded his head, mouthing back that he was tired and was going to open his door.

"No!' I screamed, dropping my phone. I had fumbled around looking for it, but he was out of the car before I finally grabbed it. I stared in horror waiting for him to explode or something. My scream had awakened the entire car and I looked over to see both twins' faces pressed to the glass.

"Mommy, the man just got out the car. Can we get out too?" I was still holding my breath, waiting for something to happen.

The man turned to me. Through the glass, he tried to describe how the air felt. "It's not regular air, but it's breathable. The ground is soft, and there is this green stuff, grass maybe," We all watched him bend over and touch the ground. He pulled up some of the green stuff that resembled moss. "The ground is squishy, but it's also kind of wet, like..."

"A tongue!" Imani screamed.

24

The man investigated. "Yah, the texture of the ground does feel somewhat like a—" Before he could finish his sentence, he was gone. We looked out the window and saw him being lifted into the air with his feet dangling above our car. I attempted to peer out the window and saw something had him suspended in the air. Suddenly, the man fell directly onto the hood of our car.

We all screamed. The entire top of the man's head was gone. His brain was gone. *He* was gone. We couldn't stop screaming. And the immediate cars around us were screaming as well. *What could have done this?* In my 34 years, nothing could have possibly prepared me for such an atrocious moment.

"Keep your hands and face away from the window," I heard my husband say as calmly as he could. "Imani, pass that plastic bag to your brother. After that, hand me that bat in the back. Babe... Babe! Please stop screaming." I didn't even realize I had still been screaming until he said it. My husband was giving everyone instructions, and I was just trying to remember how to breathe. Deronn puked into the plastic bag, almost on cue. "Babe, I need to lay your chair all the way back, so I can reach across you and access your window. I'm going to roll it down and push that man off our hood with the bat."

I was shaking so much, I could hardly respond or follow his directions. I was terrified at the thought of my husband opening the window, but I couldn't even open my mouth to articulate it. I watched him reach over and crank the car, so he could roll down the window. My heart sped up and I grabbed his arm to stop him. He gave me a reassuring look and I held my breath, watching the window go down. His attempts to push the man off the car at an awkward angle was the longest two minutes of my life, but after three failed attempts, he was finally able to do it. The man slid off our car and plopped somewhere near the front. He pulled the bat back into the car and we all saw the blood dripping from the tip. Instinctively, Imani handed her dad a wipe, and Deronn threw up again.

My husband communicated with the woman in the car closest to him. Her name was Lupe and she had gotten a better view of whatever had grabbed the man. He rolled his window down an inch, and she did the same. She appeared to be in her fifties and had a heavy Spanish accent. My mother-in-law was from Panama and my husband spoke Spanish fluently. Noticing her accent, he asked if it would be easier to communicate in Spanish? Lupe let out a sigh of relief and started giving him more details in Spanish, describing a fish the size of a man. It had shiny dark scales and wings that wrapped around it like a bat. That was all she was able to see before it dropped the man and flew away. *Bat-like wings? Maybe we were all in a cave somewhere.* That would explain the bats, the darkness, and the moss. But it wouldn't explain the rows of teeth. Frustrated, I kept trying to figure out what was going on while my husband and Lupe continued to talk. Then, the car started moving again.

With just our windows down, we were able to communicate with about five cars around us. All at once, everyone began to speculate about what they thought was going on.

"We fell into a cave in the ocean!"

"We were swallowed by a whale. Like Moby Dick. Or the one in the Bible!"

"Aliens!"

"This is some government shit!"

"The wrath of God!"

"Aliens!"

Aliens seemed to be the most popular choice, but nobody really knew anything, so everything was just speculation. And no one had any service. The cave thing seemed sort of plausible, but there was no explanation for the bat-fish that Lupe had seen. *Were there more?*

The car moved again and we heard more screams. I stopped everyone who was talking and looked down at my husband's watch. "Every couple hours our cars shift forward and people scream. Is no one else noticing this?" A few people said they heard a few screams, but no one had felt the cars move. I was beginning to think I was trippin'. Suddenly, everyone started to hear the screams, and then, there was more screaming. Lupe said that she had heard the screams before, but ignored them. We were all terrified and confused. I started to wonder if the screaming came from people who got swooped up by the bat-fish.

The screaming still hadn't stopped and we started to get even more worried. To make matters worse, we started to bicker. The kids from three of the cars were hungry and only two families had food. I could not concentrate on food, because I felt like everyone should have been paying more attention to the cars moving. And now, the kids were yelling that they had to go pee.

Suddenly, the screaming finally stopped—so suddenly, it shocked everyone. Lupe and my husband started speaking Spanish in a rapid manner, and everyone seemed to start freaking out worse than before.

* * *

Two hours after the screaming ended, things had calmed down a bit. We decided to divide all our food amongst the five cars, allowing the kids to eat first. We all had our windows cracked for communication and air circulation, but no one dared to roll

27

them down all the way. We were all praying that our car would serve as a barrier between us and whatever the hell was out there. We had also developed a bathroom routine within our car. It was gross, but sufficient. After barely finishing relieving myself, I felt the car lurch forward. I looked around and saw similar reactions from the others. We had all felt it. Two cars away, a man started to tell us that he felt the cars moving forward, but he couldn't finish his statement because the screaming started again. Everyone fell silent. We had to figure out what was causing the cars to move forward and why the screaming always followed. *What was the connection?*

The screaming went on for about an hour and half. During that time, we tried to strategize. We thought about sending someone out to investigate, hoping that it might get us somewhere, but no one volunteered. One car ahead, a woman suggested that we draw straws. The person with the shortest straw would have to leave the car to investigate what was going on.

I was opposed to it all. Based on my calculations, we had been inside this cave for almost 24 hours, and surely someone would be looking for hundreds of cars. If we just waited, someone would find us. As I pled my case to my husband, I recognized that look on his face. Before I could say anything, my husband volunteered to go.

"Are you out of your mind?" I protested. "What about the kids? What about me? We all saw what that thing did to the guy next to us. You're straight trippin' if you think I am going to let you go out there and die!"

My husband quietly waited for me to finish. "I know you are scared. So am I. But we need to figure out what's happening. For all we know, we might be inside an enormous machine, and we just need to reconfigure things to get out."

28

Tears started to form. "But we don't know. What we do know is that there are living beings in this thing and you haven't fully healed from your accident last spring. You wouldn't be stealthy at all. Stop trying to be a hero and let someone else go. We know nothing about those things or where we are. No. Just no!"

He gently rubbed my temple. "Sitting here waiting for our car to move isn't helping. We are running out of food and water, and it's only a matter of time before those things get bold enough to approach someone's car. We're sitting ducks. I'm going." His mind was made up.

For the next forty-five minutes, he and and the other cars came up with a plan to get him out of the car safely. They gave him some of their supplies, including a flashlight and a knife. We put each of the items inside Imani's backpack for him to use. The twins had fallen back asleep, and he was going to take the opportunity to sneak out his window into Lupe's car and out the back of her SUV. As he finished up with her, I decided to slide out my window and into the dead man's car.

By the time my husband noticed what I had done, I was already in the passenger seat. "What the hell do you think you're doing?" he whispered loudly. "Get back over here!"

"No! I am much more suited for this mission. Plus, I studied speleology briefly in college. If we are in a cave, I might be able to figure something out. And if we aren't, I'm still in a better position to help. I can do this."

Anger, and then fear, filled his face. "Babe, this is not one of your experiments. This isn't even brain surgery. This is you putting your life on the line. The kids need their mother!"

I nodded. "They need their father as well. If those things come back here, I know you would think fast and move smart for our children. I can do this. I know I freaked out earlier, but it was only because a dead man fell on our car! I am good now. I promise." I could see the fear in his eyes. It was a look I hadn't seen since the twins were born.

He shook his head. "I know you can do this. I remember when you performed surgery on that baby's brain and put it back inside its mother's womb. Ever since then, I've known you could do anything. I just don't want to watch you die." Even with in the faintest light, I could see tears on his face. He hadn't cried in years.

He held up both of his hands to sign. When we first started dating, we were in college, taking a sign language class together. The first time he asked me out, he signed it to me. I originally replied with a no before agreeing to go out with him. Since then, whenever we couldn't speak the words to one another, we used sign language.

"You better keep your ass safe," he signed. I blew him a kiss, grabbed the backpack and slid out the dead man's driver side door.

There was not a lot of room between the dead man's driver's side door and the next car, but I was able to slide onto the ground. I saw what the man meant when he said it felt like a tongue. It wasn't quite as wet, but it definitely didn't feel like cement. I took the opportunity to look up at the ceiling of whatever we were in. I couldn't see anything, but darkness. I started to wonder if the bat-fish could see heat in the dark. They might not be able to see us through cars, but they would certainly be able to see outside the car. My best option was to army crawl under and between cars. Most of them were facing the same direction, so I decided to just follow the cars forward.

I had only gone between four cars, when I heard a sound. Almost as soon as I heard it, it went away. I continued to army crawl between and under the cars. My elbows were starting to get sore, and my arm still had a low throb from earlier. *How did soldiers do this?* I was halfway between two cars when I recognized the noise from earlier. *Was that flapping?* I hurried to slide under the next car. I waited and listened. I heard nothing but silence, but I had an eerie feeling that something else was waiting in silence as well. It felt like I was being hunted.

I slowly slipped my hand into my bag and pulled out an orange. I knew this wasn't the time to waste any food, but I had to see if I was right. I rubbed the orange against my skin to warm it up. If the bat-fish noticed heat signatures, they might not go for a room temperature orange, but I had to try something.

After about five minutes, I slid the orange out of my shirt. My plan was to gently roll the orange to the front of the car. Hopefully there would be enough room for whatever that thing was to grab it and reveal itself. I held my breath. *I can do this.* I gently rolled the orange towards the front of the car, but it didn't quite make it, rolling right to the edge of the car. I slid the knife out of Imani's backpack and army crawled closer to the front, poking the orange forward as hard as I could. It rolled in front of the car and I waited for something to grab it. But nothing happened. No talons, claws, or wings appeared. *What is it waiting for? Grab the orange!*

"Was that for me?" My eyes grew wide as a most peculiar voice pierced the air. I told myself that it was just my imagination. I had to have imagined that voice. It was unlike any human voice I had heard before. Suddenly, a shadowy figure stood to the right of me between the cars. "No really, was that for me?" I began to shake beneath the car. "Surely you didn't think a clementine could ever take the place of a brain?" It bent down so that its face was the same level as mine. I grabbed the flashlight, but struggled to turn it on. "Not sure you want to do that. It might cause you to scream or pass out, and both would be a nuisance for me." I turned the flashlight on and the sight made me pass out.

* * *

When I came to, my neck was at an awkward position. The light was still on and as soon as my eyes cleared, I began to scream. It didn't exactly have a fish face, but it looked like some kind of aquatic creature. Regardless, it was terrifying. "Yes, I'm still here. And still annoyed by your human screams!" it said with a sigh. "Don't bother trying to make it to another car—you're going to die at some point anyway. Come, let's just make this easier for both of us." I decided to make a break for it. I rolled under the next car and started to roll towards another car, when I was met by another presence. *This can't be the same creature.*

Almost reading my mind, I heard its voice. "Surely you didn't think there was just one of us? Humans have always been so limited in thinking. There are several of us... and we're hungry. Although feasting on the brains of humans seems like a cognitive set back." Snickers and chuckles filled the space. I counted at least four separate sounds. "I'm sure you're trying to figure out a plan. Your heart is racing and your mind is going in circles. But I can personally assure you that there is no way out. Even if you happen to slip past us, there is no way out of this vessel."

"Vessel?" I whispered.

"So, you *can* talk? Tell me, what possessed you to get out of the safety of your car and roll under these cars? Where were you going? If anything, you should have gone the other way—the direction you are headed towards is imminent death." More snickers and laughter erupted in the air.

I cleared my throat. "Where are we? And what are you?"

I must have been a comedian, because more laughter came from around the car. "Does it matter? No, really... does it matter? I could go into great detail about how we predate most prehistoric creatures, how we are the children of fallen gods, and how this vessel allows us to take refuge because we get rid of the garbage... but what would be the fun in that? You are going to die with that knowledge."

I concluded that the creatures either didn't have the physical strength to lift the car or their body prohibited it somehow. Whatever the case was, if they could have gotten to me, they would have already done it. I decided to wait it out. I glanced at my husband's watch and knew I had another hour until the screaming and imminent death began again. I would just wait and hope that I didn't slide from under the car to their grasp.

I waited and waited. And this time I didn't fall asleep. Something about the air inside the vessel made me sleepy. It was some type of gas, no doubt. I checked the watch and saw that we were getting closer. There were only fifteen minutes left until the screaming would begin again. The creatures had been completely quiet, for they knew the screaming was coming as well.

As I moved to adjust myself, the car started to slide and I slid with it. Something was wrong. This was too early and I wasn't ready. I tried desperately to grab hold of something, but I found myself at a weird angle and I couldn't grab onto anything beneath the car. *Shit!* I grabbed a huge patch of green moss. I was slipping but able to hold on. I looked behind me and knew that the creatures were waiting for me to slide out from under the car. The car ahead bumped into mine and my hand let go. I slid out from under the car momentarily before grabbing onto some moss by the front tire, but by then it was too late. One of the bat-fish grabbed my leg and started to pull. The tug-of-war went on for only a few minutes. Though they were very strong, their wings prevented them from grasping my leg with a solid grip. I could fight it off by kicking with my other leg, but my angle was so funky, I would have to let go and reposition, which would leave me vulnerable for the creature to pull me out further. I was too scared to let go of the moss, but I didn't see any other choice. Preparing for the worst, I moved to release it from my grasp, when I heard a commotion. I looked as much as I could to see what was going on. *Was that a flare? What in the hell?* Suddenly, the bat-fish let go of my leg. I immediately slid my leg back under the car and changed my position. Above me, all I heard were shrieks. I wanted to poke my head out and get a better view, but I didn't dare.

A few moments passed before an unfamiliar voice asked me if I was ok. I looked to my immediate left and saw a human hand reaching for me. "It's ok, you can come out now. We scared most of them off." Hesitantly, I slid out from under the vehicle. Standing before me was a teenage boy, who couldn't have been older than 18. He had beautiful dark skin, freckles, and orange hair.

"Thank you." That was all I could really muster out. My heart was still racing.

With an Irish accent, the young man turned to two other boys who looked about his age and gave them some type of instruction. *A Black Irishman?* At some point, he started talking to me again, but I was completely oblivious. "Miss? Miss!"

I snapped out of it. "Yes, sorry. I'm still trying to get my thoughts together."

He put his hands on my shoulder. "I know you are scared. We are too. We're supposed to be hiking in the Redwoods right now, not fighting for our lives. But we're all here together... in this wild situation. And I need you to snap out of it."

I looked into his sincere eyes as he delivered his message. Hearing his voice crack, made me wonder how old he really was. He was small in stature and wore baggy clothes. Though he was smaller than his companions, he was clearly the leader. *Oh Lord. I'm about to take directions from a baby.*

"Do you know what's going on? Or where we are? Those creatures said we were in a vessel. Do you know what that means?"

He shook his head. "I have no certainty about anything. All I know is that wherever we are, there's a lava pit that eats cars."

As the boys explained what eating the cars meant, I tried to discern what they were saying, but I couldn't. "Can you take me there?" Everyone stopped in their tracks.

With an equally thick Irish accent, one of the boys who had been quiet spoke out. "Miss, we barely made it out of that lava pit and you want us to go back? Are you out of your mind?" I understood their sentiments. They were trying to get away from the lava, but something told me it was a clue. I needed to go there if I was going to figure out how to save my family.

"I get it. Just point me in the direction." All of them pointed in the direction I needed to go with a few details on what to expect. After gearing up to head that way, the boys hugged me fiercely.

The leader put on a brave face and gave me his lantern and two flares. "Stay safe, Miss." And then they were gone, disappearing in between cars, going the opposite direction as I started towards the lava.

I had been walking for about twenty minutes when I heard the

35

fluttering. *Damn. They were back.* I needed to get under a car and quick. I saw a van that looked like I would have enough room to maneuver underneath if need be. As I started to scoot under, the door opened and a man told me to get in. Since I only had seconds before those things swooped down, I got inside.

Before I had a chance to open my mouth to say thank you, a woman grabbed for my backpack. "Whoa, whoa! This belongs to me!" Looking around, I counted the woman, a man and three children. "I don't mind sharing what I have, but don't grab at anything of mine! I'm grateful for the refuge and I will see what I can part with—but the children come first." I started to unzip my backpack and noticed some weird-ass energy. The man and woman were nearly drooling as I opened my backpack, while the kids kept their head down. They were quiet. *Too quiet.* I gave everyone in the car a piece of fruit.

While they ate, I took the opportunity to examine the situation. They had all the inside car lights on, so I was able to study everyone. Something was definitely off. The kids seemed scared. As I continued to try and figure things out, the woman demanded more fruit.

"I need the rest. I have no more to spare."

"Well, then it seems you've served your purpose," she said with the weirdest grin on her face. She opened the door and I slid out. There was something off about the whole family, but unfortunately, I could not stick around to find out what it was.

I took one more glance at the oldest child who had lifted his head to meet my gaze. His eyes were pleading with me. "I'll be back if I find some food." Something was going on with those children, but it was the best I could do and I felt terrible that I couldn't help more.

I slid under another vehicle. I was still being hunted. One of

36

bat-fish landed nearby. "Round two?" A chorus of chuckles rang out. *Shit, the same thing is about to happen.* The screaming, the sliding and the creatures grabbing me. I looked around. There wasn't any of the thick green moss to hold onto and the Irish teens were long gone. I was screwed. Remembering I had the flares, I decided to wait until the screaming began to slide out, but that was the full extent of my plan. If I ever got back to my lab, I was going to make an amazing trauma test subject.

I was freaking out as quietly as possible, trying to think of a solution. *Wait, the knife!* I frantically searched my pockets and realized I had left it under the other car. I was defenseless. As I readied myself to slide, I felt the car move, but I hadn't heard any screams. *Why was the car moving?* Peering from underneath the vehicle, I saw the bat-fish shaking the car. *Were they trying to tip it over?* They were strong and I could feel the car starting to give. Looking around, I could see that they had me surrounded. There was no way I could make it to another car without one of them seeing me. I couldn't wait until the cars started moving to slide out, and now I was feeling like my flare idea wasn't very wise. There was only one creature at the back of the vehicle. I moved close and turned the lantern on. I studied its feet. It really looked like an aquatic bat. I thought for a moment, if they're used to flying, maybe their legs were weak? I decided to test my theory. I pulled the lantern back as far as I could and swung it directly into the creature's feet.

The shriek the bat-fish let out was comparable to the one I heard earlier when the group of teens had attacked. I had to move quickly. Rolling over to another side, I did the same to another creature. And then another. They began to communicate with each other with a series of clicks. They must have been warning each other because I wasn't able to get to the last one.

"Smart, human. But you missed one and now, you've made us all mad!" With more fury, all the creatures started shaking the car again. The first one hadn't made it to the back of the car yet, so I took the opportunity to roll under the next car and then rolled under another. I could still hear them shaking the car and decided to use my flare. I stood up and out in the open, hoping they would be afraid and fly away.

However, they turned from the car and started towards me. "You thought your little friends frightened us with lights? You're so simple. They had knives and weapons." *That makes more sense.* Before long, I was surrounded and closed my eyes, bracing myself for what was going to come next. If they were going to eat my brain, I refused to watch.

Suddenly, I heard a murmuring hum. *Was that growling?* I opened my eyes and standing before me was a giant leopard. *How the hell did a leopard get in here?* The creatures clicked to each other and decided to test out the new enemy. Two of the creatures jumped onto the giant cat, and within seconds, both their throats were torn out. The leopard turned to the other two creatures daring them to try, but they didn't want any smoke. Both flew straight into the air until all I could hear were distant flaps.

Not knowing what my fate was, I decided to stand as still as possible. I closed my eyes again. A few moments passed and I opened an eye. Standing before me was the little boy from the van. He was naked and had a tail that was disappearing in front of my eyes. I went to give him my hoodie and had barely made it to him before he passed out in my arms. I had to get him somewhere safe. There was a small delivery truck with a little room in between it and the next car, so I slid him there. He appeared exhausted. I reached in my bag and grabbed for my water.

He rested for several minutes before he was able to open his mouth. "We need help. My sisters are like me. We are all in danger." With much exertion, the little boy told me his story. He and his siblings had been taken away from their parents after ICE raided a house they were living in with relatives. He and his siblings were able to get away using their ability. He said they were *Blessed*. I didn't know what any of it meant, but I was right to suspect there was something going on. They weren't his parents—they were holding him and his sisters hostage. They had put a device on one of his sisters so she couldn't transform.

It was so much to take in, I decided not to focus on the magical part. "How did you all even get caught up with these two?"

The boy's eyes teared up. "Our parents told us if we ever got lost to find a church. We found one that sheltered us for a while. But one day, my baby sister transformed in front of a group of other kids. The next thing we knew, we were being handed over to two men. Before we were swallowed, they were taking us to a dealer who purchases the *Blessed*."

I could tell the earlier transformation had taken a lot from him. "How can I help?"

"Please go back to the van," he said with his eyes closed. "The man keeps the chain to my sister's collar around his neck." Just that quickly, he fell asleep. I hid him underneath the truck and prepared for the worse.

* * *

I crept up to the van and looked around. Everyone appeared to be asleep. I gently knocked against the window and opened the door as the man popped his head up. "You again? What the hell do you want?"

I could see the chain around his neck. "I saw the boy that was in the van earlier! He ran past me. I can show you where he went!"

Looking me up and down, he turned to the woman and whispered something in her ear. "It isn't worth it!" she said. "We will get a nice amount just for these two! Just get back in!"

The man looked annoyed that the woman had replied out loud. "Shut up and keep an eye on these two."

The woman sat back clearly dismayed. Looking at me, she smiled. "If anything happens to him, I won't hesitate to kill both of these little girls." I had no doubt.

The older sister jumped up and hugged me. As she squeezed me, I took the opportunity to whisper something in her ear. She sat back and acknowledged what I said with her eyes.

Walking with the man was scary. I didn't know what he was capable of, but I knew he kidnapped little children and that was all I needed to know. "Where is he?" he questioned. "I feel like we've been walking in circles!" I kept walking without answering. I didn't know what to say and I was a terrible liar. "Hey bitch! Did you hear me?" Turning around, he placed his hand on a gun that had been hidden in his waist. "I'm not going any further until you tell me where he is! I know you know and I will shoot you where you stand if you don't speak right now. TALK!" His screaming didn't scare me. It was the attention that his voice brought that scared me. He reached for his gun and grabbed my wrist. Struggling to pull away from him, I heard the flapping. *Oh no. Not now.* Swiftly, one of the bat-fish swooped down to grab him and I felt my feet leaving the ground. *So, this is what it feels like to fly.*

The man had a death grip on my wrist and we were both in the air. I did the only thing I could think of: I quickly swung my full weight around in an effort to try and grab the chain from around his neck. I missed and worried that the man could drop me at any given moment, but I refused to let that happen without getting that chain. I swung again and missed. *Damn. Third time's a charm. Crap! Maybe a fourth?*

I swung my body as much as I could to leverage my weight against gravity, and despite the awkward angle, I finally grabbed his chain. I almost wanted to cry, until I realized that I was still going higher in the air. By now the man was fighting for his life with the creature. At some point, he must have remembered he had a gun because he let me go to reach for it.

I fell on top of a car. Knowing I had been high enough that the impact had probably damaged something, but there was no time to nurse my wounds. I had to get back to the girls. I attempted to stand up and fell over. Something was wrong with my wrist and ribs. If I had the proper aid, I could wrap myself. Leaning against the car, I felt dizziness take over. *Did I hit my head too?*

"Miss, miss. Are you okay?" I recognized that voice. Struggling to open my eyes, I could see the Irish teenager standing over me through blurred vision.

"I... I fell. Wrist, ribs, head. Hurt."

The teen looked me over and his face didn't look confident. "Mam, back home I was a junior lifeguard. I am CPR and first-aid certified. May I have your permission to lift your shirt and examine you?" I nodded. Very gently he looked me over. He looked up at his two companions. Instinctively, they reached into their backpacks and pulled out a first aid kit. The next few minutes were a blur. I felt sick. "Mam, it appears you broke a few ribs. It also looks like your wrist is fractured and you may have a concussion. We are going to need you to sit up—falling asleep

41

can be dangerous. Also, you have been clutching so tightly to that chain, I'm worried you might have bruised your hand. May I?" I realized I was still holding onto the man's chain and let go.

As I was helped to my feet, I tried my best to explain what was going on with the kids in the van. I needed to get back to them, but I had no point of reference. Everything looked familiar and unfamiliar at the same time. "I left the boy under a truck that said Ashe's Bread Delivery. He was in pretty bad shape, so he must still be there." A teen who had barely spoke recalled seeing the truck several cars back.

As we geared up to go, a foul smell filled the air. "We're near the lava," the leader replied, noticing my facial expression.

I had been near lava on a research trip some years ago. It had a distinct, sulfuric smell. I started to realize this wasn't lava. There was something familiar about the smell though. I had smelled something similar before. *Was it in the operating room?* I knew we needed to get back to the little boy, but I had to solve this mystery. "What's your name, sweetheart?"

The leader seemed surprised at the question. "Courtland, Miss. This is my best friend Ross and my brother Cairo."

I looked at each boy and introduced myself. "I need you to get this chain to that little boy."

Courtland frowned. "There's no way we are leaving you again. Look at your condition. We have to do this together, so you can solve this mystery once and for all."

We started towards the strange smell. While walking, I told the boys what I did and why the smell seemed familiar. Cairo pointed out that we were right by the lava. I turned the lantern towards the smell. I crept as close as I could to examine it. Most of the cars were half melted and some were abandoned. The ones that weren't had people inside that were slumped over. *Were they dead or sleeping?* The smell was giving me a headache. I took down my head wrap to cover up my nose and mouth. I used a few locs to tie the rest of my hair back. Suddenly, I recognized the smell. It was familiar because we all had it inside of us—it was bile. My family had been right all along. We were in some type of creature, a creature big enough to swallow an entire bridge of cars.

I needed a moment to think, but I couldn't do it with the bile smell lingering in the air. I started to realize that the closer you were to the bile, the sleepier you became. The bile must have been releasing some type of gas that caused exhaustion.

I started to head in the opposite direction, away from the gas.

"Miss, what did you find out?" I was so lost in my thoughts that I didn't hear Ross talking to me. I had to get that collar off and free those girls. "Miss!"

Courtland stepped directly in front of me, snapping me from my thoughts. "I'm sorry. I have a lot going through my mind right now."

Courtland nodded. "Care to share your thoughts?"

I explained that the lava was actually bile, a fluid from the bottom of our stomachs. I told them that the creature was using it to digest its food and releasing some type of gas.

"So, it's not lava at all?"

I shook my head. "No. It's the creatures stomach acid. When the cars move forward, it means the creature has digested more cars. The screaming must have been from the poor souls melting to death. We have to warn the others."

We weren't too far from the truck where I had left the boy. They were speaking excitedly to each other about how we were going to get out. Most of their ideas were terrible and involved tools we didn't have. I could see the truck. Walking swiftly, I

43

bent down to see if he was still under there and he was. His breathing seemed to have returned to normal and he appeared to be in a deep sleep. Now, I needed to rescue his sisters.

I remembered how to get back to the van, but I was nervous. The woman seemed unpredictable and the girls were limited in what they could do out of fear. Courtland had chosen to accompany me and pointed out blood on the side of the van. Even from a distance, I could see a bloody handprint on the window. I nodded and motioned for him to remain quiet. Creeping up to the van, I could see one of the sisters. The one with the collar was covered in blood and shaking.

"Where is your sister and the woman?" I asked. Without lifting her head, she pointed behind me. I turned to look and saw the most beautiful black leopard I had ever seen eating, what I could only assume, was the woman's remains. Its shiny coat was black and covered with even darker spots than the rest of the coat. Carefully, I walked to the large cat. The cat instinctively raised its head and growled its disapproval at me. "Easy, easy. You are doing such a great job taking care of your sister. I'm glad you took the opportunity to defend yourself. I have the key to unlock her collar. May I?" The cat seemed to understand me and gave a nod of approval.

As I approached the little girl to take the collar off, a loud noise stopped all of us. "What the hell is going on here?" The man had returned and shot his gun into the air. He must have won his fight with the bat-fish. "Where is Lydia and that sister of yours? And who are you?"

Before Courtland could speak up, I stepped in front of the situation. "I'm sure you can see the blood and assume what might have happened. What I have right here is the key from around your neck. Two of the children are in their cat form and

44

ready for you to make a move. Regardless, I will be unlocking her collar." I prayed he wouldn't call my bluff. He started to look around frantically. The sister cat was nowhere to be found, but I knew she was near.

"You know, you have been causing all kinds of trouble ever since we let you into our van. Why did you have to come along and mess up our good thing?"

"Your good thing?" I scoffed. "You are a human trafficker. You're a monster!"

He pointed the gun directly at me. "I'm not a monster. *They are.* They're not even human!"

I closed my eyes and waited. The man screamed. The older sister cat had bit him in the leg, forcing him to drop his gun and I went to grab it. "That's enough. You already fed once today." The sister cat growled at me but obliged. Holding the gun shakily, I gave the key to Courtland to release the girl.

The man was writhing in pain and put his hands up. "The collar is on her for a reason. She isn't like the others! She is dangerous. That collar is for everyone's protection. You have to believe me."

I didn't trust him, assuming he would say anything to keep his bounty. I turned towards the sister cat, who had already begun the transformation back into her human form. "Is there any truth to what he is saying?"

Her eyes still looked like cat eyes. "Yes. But she wouldn't be a danger to you. Just to him and others like him." I didn't have a lot of time to contemplate and my gut was telling me to let her go. I gave a slight nod to Courtland and he released her.

The little girl stepped out of the van. She walked up to the man and spit on him. She walked to her sister and asked about their brother as the man screamed. Heading towards the truck,

I quickly explained what was going on. "I need to put you in a safe place. I need you all to remain hidden." I had an idea, but I couldn't babysit in the process.

* * *

"Wait. You want to do what?"

I took a pen and paper out of the bag, fully prepared to break it down to Courtland. "If this vessel is as old as I think it is, its stomach probably hasn't encountered certain things. I want to give it a stomachache, so it'll throw up."

After seeing two of the bat-fish get their throats torn out, it appeared the others had been frightened off as well. Feeling that we were finally safe from their attacks, we decided to seek help from some of the people still taking up shelter nearby inside their cars. Courtland and his crew seemed completely on board with the plan.

For the next two hours, we unloaded everything we could think of into the stomach acid. We dumped tires, toys, car seats, teddy bears, cheese and all the dead bodies we could find. Nothing was working. The vessel appeared completely unmoved. Not long after, the three *Blessed* children came out of hiding. They wanted to help, but I couldn't think of anything else we could do. Nothing seemed to disrupt this vessel's stomach. Besides that, we were all standing too close to the bile and I felt myself getting dizzy from the fumes.

As we gathered our stuff to retreat, I heard a familiar voice. "Mommy!"

Turning around to see the twins and my husband should have brought some joy, but before I knew what was happening, one of the bat-fish swooped down to grab Imani and everything became a blur. My husband held onto her as tight as he could, and soon, they were both being lifted into the air. I stood there, completely frozen. *What's wrong with me? I am going to lose my daughter and I can't even move.*

Suddenly, I heard commotion from behind. I didn't dare think of turning around, because all I could focus on was my husband's legs getting smaller and smaller as he and Imani went higher and higher into the darkness. Finally finding my voice, I screamed for them both, but my legs still wouldn't move even as Deronn was screaming my name. Without warning, something furry brushed against my body and flew into the air.

I assumed that it was another bat-fish at first, but it looked odd. As it flew higher into the air, I saw that it resembled the two leopards I had seen earlier, but was golden with white spots, a long tail, and beautiful wings. As it disappeared into the darkness, I heard the familiar shrieks of the bat-fish. I then saw a blinding light, resembling some type of fire.

After a while, I was finally able to move into action. I grabbed Deronn and shoved him into a car. I called out to a group that had mentioned having blankets earlier. I needed three others to help me hold the blankets in place just in case someone fell from the sky. I looked beside me and saw two leopards standing guard, ensuring our protection from any other bat-fish. Suddenly, I saw my husband falling. I screamed for everyone to hold tight to the blanket. He came in fast against the edge of the blanket, which lessened his fall, but still ended up hitting his shoulder atop a car. Once I noticed that he seemed to be okay, my eyes returned to the sky. *Where was my baby girl?* Looking up, all I could see were bursts of light. *What is going on up there?*

Almost suddenly, the shrieking and the light stopped. My heart stopped as well. *Where is Imani? Where is my baby?* Tears

47

started to fill my eyes. I couldn't even check on my husband, because I kept looking up, hoping she would drop. Suddenly, someone yelled. A man with a yellow shirt pointed into the air. I squinted but couldn't quite make out what I was seeing. I could only tell that it was getting closer.

After a few more moments, I saw that it was the flying leopard, and in her mouth, was Imani with her eyes closed and blood on her shirt. As the leopard set her down, I ran to check her pulse. Imani was still alive, but I could tell there was something wrong with the leopard. She appeared to be having a hard time breathing and kept coughing up stuff. With a loud hack, she spewed a golden acid-like substance. The blast was fiery and covered a long distance. Some of it hit the vessel's bile, and we saw it bubble beneath the leopard's acid.

Courtland was the first person to voice his surprise. "Did you see that?"

Turning to the leopard, I asked her if she understood me. With a soft growl, she nodded her head. "I need you to cough or sneeze... or whatever you just did... into the vessel's bile." The leopard looked confused, but walked closer to the edge before spewing a gallon of the fiery acid into the creature's bile. This time it caused a considerable reaction, forcing a wave of bile to rise up and crash down on the nearby cars. Finally, I had a plan.

We needed to get all the people into cars as far away as possible. I had already concluded that we must have been some of the last cars swallowed. We were probably close to opening of the mouth. We all started searching the empty cars and our own cars for supplies. We split into three teams with one leopard joining each group. After gathering what we could, we piled into the biggest vehicles we could find and moved on to the next step of the plan.

Standing on top of a car, I got everyone's attention. "In order for this to work, we really need to stick to the plan. We wait until we get pushed out, and we stay in our cars the shortest duration of time possible. And this is all contingent on if the creature spits us out at the surface. If we are spit out at the ocean's bottom, then we are doomed. For those with small children, be sure to give them the water bottle snorkels we've created. It won't last long, so they will absolutely need help getting to the surface. We are all hoping that we are close to the shore or that the military is outside waiting for us. Regardless, we will die if we remain here. If not by the stomach acid, those bat-fish will surely try their best to pick us off." Looking around at the worried faces, I felt doomed. We had no idea what was waiting for us outside the vessel. For all we knew, we were going to spit out off the coast of Japan. We were all scared, and the air (or lack thereof) seemed to be getting worse. We were only left with one choice.

As we geared up and went over the plan again, some families decided to stay: an elderly man with a disabled son, a mother and her two kids, and a few others. I respected their decision. This was dangerous and none of us knew what would happen next. One of the leopards escorted them to the back of the throat, towards the bile. They all got into cars and waited to be digested.

The flying leopard got into position. She was directly above the bile, fluttering back and forth. We were all scared as hell, waiting at what we assumed was the entrance to the vessel's mouth. *Why couldn't it have swallowed a truck full of aquatic gear?* In two minutes, we would all press loudly on our car horns, signaling the leopard to spew its acid into the vessel's bile. We hoped this would trigger some type of reaction causing the vessel to open its mouth and vomit us out. I was terrified. My husband and a few other people had taken the engines and heaviest parts out of

49

the cars in hopes that they would float easier, but at this point, nothing was guaranteed.

It was time. I glanced from car to car, then at the leopards, then my kids, and finally my husband. I knew I needed to press the horn, but I hesitated. *Press it. Damn it, Nzinga—press the damn horn!* My heart continued to beat quickly until I finally laid my hand on the horn as hard as I could.

It seemed like forever before we saw fiery sparks from a distance. The leopard spewed her acid and the first wave of bile rose up and hit the cars in front of us. My heart pounded, hoping the vessel would release us before the bile hit our car. The leopard would also need time to fly into our car and I wasn't sure if any of my calculations could be exact. The bile was starting to get closer to us, but the vessel had not yet opened its mouth to let us out. *Come on. Come on. We don't have a Plan B.*

The leopard spewed for a bit longer and then flew to our vehicle at top speed. She slid in across the laps of the twins and her siblings. I looked back at all their little faces. *If we survive this and I can't find their parents, I guess our family just got a little bigger.* I turned back and saw that the bile was still getting closer. *This isn't going to work. Damn it!* I turned to my husband and kissed his hand, signing how much I loved him. He lifted his hands to do the same, when the car began to shake. We turned around and saw what had to be rows of teeth coming into view. We hadn't anticipated just how many rows there were. Regardless, the vessel had finally decided that it wanted us out.

The next few minutes were utterly terrifying. It was like we were on a roller coaster ride, except the end was certain death. At one point, we smashed directly into a tooth and I thought the car was going to tear in half. I was too afraid to see how everyone fared from the impact, and with the rushing of water and bile all around us, I didn't have time to care. It seemed like it took forever, but we were finally in water.

It was dark, so we were either at the bottom of the ocean or it was nighttime. *Please let this car float.* Slowly, the car started drifting towards the surface. As it got closer, we saw light. We finally reached the surface, but the car was still submerged. As planned, we were going to have to bust the windows out and get everyone to the top of the car. The twins could swim, but the *Blessed* children could not. This was going to be tricky because we had very little time before the car would be completely filled with water, and for this to work, nothing could go wrong.

My husband busted the passenger side window. As quickly as possible, he guided our children to the top of the car. I grabbed the *Blessed* children one by one and brought them to the top. As I got to the middle sister, she seemed to be tugging away from me. *What the hell? Is she still buckled in? Why can't I pull her out?* I squinted my eyes trying to see why she was stuck and my eyes widened with horror. One of the bat-fish was in my back seat, holding her in place. It must have gotten in when I was putting her brother on top of the car. I only had thirty seconds left before I needed air, but I was too scared to go back up without her. Without thinking, I went for its beady little eyes, jabbing the creature with my wedding ring. I didn't hear it shriek, but I was certain I had wounded it based on the way it contorted its mouth. The bat-fish finally let go of the girl and I took the opportunity to grab her. I forced us both towards the surface and on top the top of the car, blacking out as soon as I inhaled my first breath of fresh air.

* * *

When I came to, everyone was hovering over me. I tried to sit up. "What happened?" I asked.

My husband shook his head. "Those things came for us. We were able to pull you out of the water, but some of the others weren't so lucky." I looked around and saw at least ten other cars with people seated on top. We had started with seventeen. I looked for Courtland and saw that he and his crew were safe. I attempted to study our surroundings. Nothing looked familiar and I couldn't see land anywhere. I laid back down. *Now what?*

Suddenly, a loud horn rang out. *Was it a rescue boat? The coast guard?* I sat up excitedly, and saw it was a cruise ship. At this point, I wouldn't complain—anything was better than our current situation.

It took about two hours for the ship to rescue everyone because we were so scattered across the water. After giving everyone towels to dry ourselves off, the captain asked who the leader was. I was so relieved to be safe, I nuzzled further into my towel and completely ignored what was going on around us until I heard my name again and again. I turned to see who was calling me, when I realized that everyone was naming me as the leader. *I didn't sign up for this.*

With wobbly legs, I approached the captain. "Where are we? When will we be able to go on shore?"

The captain glanced nervously at the group and then pulled me aside. "Listen, I don't want to alarm you, but you're off the coast of Greece. Clearly you all went through something down there... but as far as land goes—well, whatever you saw down there is ten times worse on land." Squinting and forcing myself not to cause a scene, I asked him to clarify. He had a thick accent and I was hoping it was the accent or some sort of language difference that was causing me to misunderstand.

"You're telling me there are more of those monsters on land? Are they just as big?"

The captain went deathly pale. "There are monsters of all shapes and sizes. And now, we're at the bottom of the food chain."

III

Part Three

"Your authentic self is valuable. As you navigate life, always remember that if you aren't being authentic, your entire being will know."

A Witch Named Compton
(Pre-apocalypse)

I wasn't absorbing everything that was going on. It could have been because of my age and lack of maturity, or simply the shrooms I had just consumed, but nothing was making sense. Once every hundred years, the witches from my circle got together to fellowship. This was my first time attending, and my anxiety was getting the best of me. We discussed everything from politics, relationships, new spells, and old. We talked about sex, money, and everything in between. These meetings sometimes went on for months. There were so many of us, that we used this time to bond, fellowship, and heal. A lot had taken place recently, and the witches that had a hand in politics were exhausted. We had to do circle rituals with them for the first two weeks at least!

There were witches everywhere. Our circle had witches from most well-known lineages: the Yadav clan, the Attakai tribe, and even the Abimbola family. You were only as strong as your lineage. Being surrounded by so many powerful witches was both exciting and intimidating. It was also lonely. I was the last one in my family still alive.

So many discussions were taking place. One especially interesting topic was the reg's obsession with referring to anything they didn't understand as witchcraft. Even if we were simply healers, if you were *Blessed*, you were a witch to humans. Within the *Blessed*, actual witches could perform most magic without spells. Even the word "witch" was a running joke in itself. The only difference between us and regs was untapped spirituality.

Legend has it that all the *Blessed* were descendants of the Abosom, lower deities from the Akan religion. Some felt that we were children of the Yoruba Orishas. Nobody knew for sure, so we all paid homage to African spirituality as a whole while practicing our own traditions in between.

Me being the youngest witch in our circle at 147 years old, I was still learning how to work my power. One thing that set me apart from others was my ability to travel between time and space. Only a few witches had ever been able to do it, and two of them were my relatives.

As I watched the elders in our circle walk around and touch the forehead of each witch, I felt my anxiety building, the closer they got to me. The elders would know that I was high. My candle was shaking in my hands. *Calm your hands, girl.* I was too young to have such bad nerves. I tried to think of a cleansing spell quickly, but I was so high, all I could think about were rainbow llamas. They were so cute with their goofy ears. *Damn it!*

An elder who had always had it out for me stopped directly in front of me. I lowered my head to receive her and waited, but nothing happened. "You dare come to this holy place, with poison from regs running through you?" Technically, shrooms were from the earth, but knowing my luck, this batch was probably laced with elephant tranquilizers. I lowered my head more. "Have you no shame, child?"

As I struggled to think of something to say, a witch named Mama Adaku intervened. She had been friends with my mother.

They both started speaking rapidly in an ancient language only they understood. I knew the conversation was getting more heated, and all I could do was wish for a swift, sudden death. I was so ashamed of myself.

"Come child, it's time for a cleansing ritual." I followed Mama Adaku to the inner cave, away from the others. I didn't dare speak first, but the silence was killing me. I knew what the cleansing ritual entailed and I was terrified. Mama Adaku lifted my lowered head. "We have no time for your shame. I need your gift." She quickly explained that she needed me to go back in time to save someone: one of her relatives who died on one of the first slave ships from West Africa heading to the Americas.

"Wait, so your relative jumped into the sea and you want me to stop her?" I didn't like this. Time travel most definitely came at a cost. And the butterfly effect was not just a theory. It was more like a "rhino effect." The results of altering the past could be disastrous to the future and she was more than aware of this.

"Please child, there isn't a lot of time. There is a war coming. We can't prevent the war, but we might be able to have a powerful witch on our side."

My head was spinning, and suddenly, I started to wish I didn't enjoy drugs so much. "You know how dangerous this is right? I could die. And the person I save could grow up to be a villain. If she was supposed to live, she would have lived. I'm not allowed to alter the past. I'm not trying to get killed by the Radar because you have some half-cocked plan to save a relative. And you said she was thirteen? That means she is eighty years away from coming into her gift. She still has to survive the plantation and we both know how many of us died at the hands of slavery discovering we were *Blessed*. This is a terrible idea."

Mama Adaku sighed. "I know this sounds wild, but I need you

59

to trust me. She was never supposed to die. She was assassinated by someone who knew what she was supposed to become." She was sounding more and more like a conspiracist. Nothing was making sense. *And what war? What was my role in this war?* The cleansing ritual was sounding more appealing by the second.

Looking at her face, I could see the seriousness in her desperation. "Why me? There are more seasoned time travelers that would be able to fulfill your request without any issues. I am a mess. I'm a poor drug addict who heals other drug addicts. I barely do powerful spells, and I have not traveled back in time since I tried to save my mother." I stopped. I couldn't continue. My heart still hurt when I thought about her. It had been a hundred years and it still felt like yesterday. Her death was so sudden and untimely, it left me with a gaping hole in my heart. Part of the reason I hadn't become a better witch was because of my 100-year depression. *I need a blunt.*

Mama Adaku waited while I processed my emotions. "Your mother was an amazing woman, and thrice the witch I am. I chose you, because you are special. And you are the only time traveler in our circle. Go back and observe the girl on the ship. I will give you a cloaking spell. You don't have to intervene if you don't want to. Just observe."

I couldn't believe I was agreeing to this. Time travel always came at a price. Lucky for me, I had nothing and no one. If I died, no one would give a shit. Maybe that was why she asked me and not another time traveler. As we quickly prepared for my departure, she gave me detailed instructions that I was only halfway listening to, because I was still high. As she continued, she hit me in the chest twice, cleansing me on the second impact. She whispered something in my ear and I began to travel.

60

* * *

Oh my god. What the hell was that smell? It literally smelled like shit. I opened my eyes and quickly covered my mouth so I wouldn't gag. Mama Adaku had knocked me into time travel. It was a method I didn't appreciate, but it got the job done. I was in a dark place surrounded by bodies. I could feel people breathing on me. *Damn, you could have at least knocked me into daytime.* I didn't feel comfortable moving around. The cloaking spell simply made me invisible to the eye. My body was still very solid and I couldn't take the chance of tripping over anyone. I assumed I was at the bottom of a slave ship. I was terrified. I couldn't see anything, but I could hear everything. A lot of whispers, and a lot of tears. I couldn't do this. I wanted to go back home.

I don't know how it happened, but at some point, I had actually managed to close my eyes and fall asleep. I was so tired, I probably could have dozed off again, but the sun had come up. I opened my eyes completely to find an older man staring at me. *How could he see me?* The cloaking spell should still be in full effect. I realized that he was actually staring through me, at something behind me. I turned and saw a group of girls in their early teens. I turned back to the dude skeptically, to make sure he wasn't being a perv. His eyes held no lust, only sadness. I stood up and hit my head on a heavy wooden bar. I bit my lip so I would not cry out. It was still really quiet and I didn't want to spook anyone.

I needed to wrap my hair up. The pretty twist-out I had preserved for the circle was shot, due to the sea-water and humidity. I quickly put my afro up into a huge bun and tiptoed over to the group. They were surrounding one girl who looked really young and were attempting to clean her up. Her face was swollen and she had tears in her eyes. I wasn't fully comprehending everything that was going on. *Was she pregnant? What the hell?* I needed to get off this damn ship.

As I prepared to time jump, I noticed one of the girls who was consoling her friend. She bent forward and I noticed a birthmark that all the witches in my family had: a half heart on the left side of our lower back. I froze and began to wonder why Mama Adaku really sent me. Why wouldn't she tell me I had a relative on the ship? And why didn't I know who this relative was? My mom had always made sure that I knew all my witch relatives, but I couldn't place her.

I studied every inch of her. Her hair, skin, and facial features. I studied her mannerisms and the worried expression as she tended to her friend. I studied her mark. The same mark we all had. I touched the one on my back to make sure it was still there like it would have suddenly disappeared while I discovered this new revelation.

I sat down. I felt around my jacket pocket for that last shroom. I couldn't do this. Whatever this was, I couldn't. I didn't know the whole story and I didn't want to make a hasty decision. I was almost positive I was sent here to save my relative, but I was puzzled that I had no idea who she was. There was a way I could go back further, but it was risky. I would have to touch my relative, and risk bringing her back with me. Everything in me told me to simply jump back to my present, but I had to know. I stuffed the shroom back into my pocket. As gently as I could, I touched my relative's shoulder.

* * *

Laughter, food, and children playing. A stern mother-like figure scolding the children. Sunshine. Happiness. I was in Africa.

I was somewhere on the coast. I could smell the sea water. I looked around for my relative, but I didn't see her. I decided to explore. Everyone seemed so content. I appeared to be in a marketplace of some sort. I kept walking towards what looked like dwellings. I had been walking for about a mile when I spotted her. She looked different. Younger. She darted into a clay-like dwelling and I quietly followed her.

As I walked inside, a warm voice greeted me. "We have been expecting you." I turned around to see if someone was behind me, because I was certain the cloaking spell was still working. "You don't need your cloaking spell here. Please sit so we can get started. We haven't got much time."

Startled and confused, I sat down and formed a triangle with my relative and the older woman who had greeted me. "Y-you can see me? How? Where am I? What is going on?"

The older woman looked at me thoughtfully and then at my younger relative. "For this spell, we needed a member of our family from the past, present, and future. We knew you would come, so here you are. Pour libations out for the ancestors and then drink this." I was confused and being handed random drinks from an elderly woman. "I know that look—you want to run away. I can tell you right now that it won't help, child. You jump, and your curiosity will eat at you. So, stay... and drink." I didn't understand anything, but I decided to drink, in hopes that I could gain some clarity, and they did the same.

Suddenly, I felt dizzy. *Was it a withdrawal from the drugs or whatever this was in this cup?* "What's going on? I saw her on a ship. She bears the birthmark that all the witches in my family have." I touched my back. Both of them touched theirs.

The elder spoke gently. "There is a lot going on right now, with very little time. From what I know about you, this won't work unless you are fully committed. We need to put a transition spell on her." She pointed to my young relative. She could have pointed to a baby pig for all I cared! A transition spell was out of the question for a young witch.

"What! A transition spell? Do you know how young I am? I don't have the power source nor the conjure energy to even bring that forth. You have the wrong witch. You should have got my mother. She was amazing. And she is still alive somewhere in this time."

The older woman shook her head. "We chose you for a reason. You are more powerful than her and you don't even realize it. You are more powerful than everyone in this room."

I rolled my eyes. "Not trying to sound disrespectful, but clearly I am more powerful than a twelve-year-old, but I highly doubt I am more powerful than you. You have to at least be 900 years old!"

They both shook their heads. "What have you heard of your relative Efua?"

I looked at them and chuckled. "That she was foolish and died a horrible death."

The older woman lowered her head. "That's fair—I did die a horrible death, but I certainly was not foolish."

The room began to spin. "Mama Efua! Had I known who I was speaking with, I would have never been so rude. Forgive me." I bowed my head and waited for forgiveness.

Mama Efua gently touched my forehead and gave me her forgiveness. "The stories you heard about me growing up most certainly have some truth to them. I died the most shameful death for witches, and it was all because I gave my loyalty to an evil king. Also, you are a few thousand years off, but I thank you for the compliment."

I needed my asthma inhaler. I also wasn't dressed for this weather. The room seemed smaller and I was having a hard time breathing. In my present, I had been in the traditional white linen dress we wore when our circle met. I had thrown my leather jacket over it because it was freezing and I didn't bring a blanket. I had also thrown on my black leather combat boots before I jumped. Now, sitting in a hut-dwelling with two of my relatives, I felt ridiculous. I knew what my mind was doing though. Whenever I am in the middle of a crisis, I focus on the random miniscule things around me. Like the big ass housefly that'd been on the wall for like an hour. "Ok, you say that you were not foolish, Maame? Can you tell me more about your death?"

She smiled. "Let me tell you more about my life. I served a king, who at the time was the most powerful king in the land. He believed in me, and in magic. He believed in the good of the people. Every bit of magic he asked of me was used to better them, whether it be for healthy crops and livestock or protection from outside forces. Because of me, he became more powerful each and every day." She stopped. Her eyes glazed over and her voice became heavy. "Then, one day he changed. Gone was the gentle, loving man I revered... and in his place, was a monstrous tyrant. He had heard about different groups turning to Christianity and started hunting these groups down. He killed so many. I had to stop him. This was not what my magic was for. This was not how magic was meant to be used. So, I struck him with blindness while he was away. The blindness was temporary, but it changed him. When he returned home, I was sure he would be humble—but instead he simply changed his enemy. Instead of Christians, he started killing off those of us with magic. He felt that his God was telling him to kill us. Because I had been his main source, he viewed me as especially dangerous, and killed me in the most dishonorable way." The tears flowed down her face. Both me and the younger relative embraced her. I don't know how long we had held her, but all of our breathing had changed. Our hearts were in tune.

Wiping her eyes with my dress, I had to know more. "Why does she need a transition spell? And what would she be transitioning to?"

For the first time, my younger relative spoke. "My name is Kukua, and I am to transition into a bonsu." *This is exactly why I enjoy drugs. For moments like this when people made ridiculous statements.*

"What? A bonsu? A whale?" My Twi was rusty, but up until then, I had understood most of what was being said. I looked from my elder to my younger relative. Both of their faces were completely serious. "I promise you both that I do not have the skillset to pull this off. You need a more seasoned witch. Possibly an elder. Literally anyone but me."

I started to get up and Kukua touched my arm. "Sit." With an adult-like seriousness, she guided me back to my place. "We don't have any more time to walk you through this. Many lives are at stake. We have approximately 39 minutes to complete this transition spell and we all need to be on the same page. Even if you don't believe in us, believe in the future. If you want there to be a future, sit down and listen." Mama Efua was quiet and watching our interaction intensely. "In one year, I will be forced onto a slave ship. One outcome is that me and a group of girls throw ourselves into the ocean and drown. The second outcome is that we throw ourselves into the ocean, I transition to my bonsu form, swallow the girls and then swim everyone to safety."

My head hurt. If I ever needed a shroom or a blunt, it was now. "Wait, wait, wait... Mama Adaku said that someone assassinated you. Was all that a lie to get me here?"

Both of my relatives looked confused. "Assassinated?" They looked at each other and then at me.

"Yes. She told me that you were never supposed to die."

Kukua shook her head. "I know nothing about an assassination. But I know that we have 35 minutes."

As I watched my relatives prepare for the ritual, I was hit with a wave of exhaustion. *Why me? Why choose me out of all the powerful witches in my lineage?* I was literally the worst, and a baby in comparison to everyone else. Jasmine was needed for the transition spell and the scent filled the room. Watching my older relative grind a bonsu tooth into a drink, I felt like I was going to pass out.

Sensing my uncertainty, Mama Efua placed her hand on my heart. "You have everything in you to do this. And if you look at it one way, you have already done this at some point in time and space." I looked over at Kukua who was burning some type of dried leaves whose smoke left a pleasant, soothing smell. I felt myself relaxing.

Kukua stopped moving the leaves around and looked at us both. "It's time."

My heart should have been beating a mile a minute, but I actually felt at peace. I wondered if there were drugs in those leaves. *Did I have contact high?* Kukua explained how we were all to be positioned for the ritual. We were to sit in a row with our legs crossed and folded inward. In addition, we all had to drink from the cup with the ground-up whale's tooth. It seemed confusing and awkward. I had never done anything like this before.

Most of my spells were petty and involved having the handcuffs of my fellow activists "miraculously" released. Many people had run away from the cops because of my handcuff trick. I also was pretty good at healing others, but a transition spell would definitely be the highlight at my next narcotics anonymous meeting.

Kukua took the lead on the ritual, asking us to concentrate and repeat certain words when necessary. She called out to the past first, asking Maame Efua for her strength and it was granted. She called out to herself, asking for strength and it was granted. In a different dialect of Twi, she called me by my name. "Compton, in this room is the past, present, and future. We need your gift, we need your voice, we need your strength." With my eyes closed, I granted Kukua's request. We all drank from the cup with the whale's tooth. It tasted gross and gritty. I closed my eyes and did my best to concentrate.

* * *

When I opened my eyes, I was back on the ship. I was confused, because it was not how my time traveling worked. I looked around for the group of girls, but they were nowhere to be found. I heard screaming close by. The door to the stairs that led to the top of the ship was open. I quickly creeped upstairs. A white man was trying to unlock the chains that held the girls together. He seemed focused on taking one in particular, the pregnant one.

Assuming that my cloaking spell was still working, I got closer to the chaos. The girls were holding on to her by wrapping themselves around her, tangling their chains and making it impossible for the man to get to her. Everyone cried and screamed as the other white men started to beat on them in an effort to release the pregnant girl. As tears flowed down my eyes, I thought about how I could intervene. I could easily push the man over the rail of the ship. If history served me correctly, sharks would be swimming close by. Examining every detail of the situation, I noticed an older woman whispering in the ear of one of the girls. For some reason, something seemed off about her and her presence was out of place. I couldn't put my finger on it, but something about her made me feel weird. *What was she whispering?* I didn't want to get too close, knowing they could still touch me, even if I was cloaked.

I tried my best to listen over the screaming, but could hear part of what she was saying. "...and all your troubles would wash away... death would be swift... all... jump!" I shrank back in astonishment. *Was this the assassin?* I had been assuming that a person with a gun shot Kukua off the ship, but the assassin was simply a manipulative old lady.

I might not have been able to physically intervene, but I could still say a few things of my own. "Stop right now, evil spirit!"

Bewildered, the assassin stopped her slithery words and looked around. "They warned me you would come. It's too late. The girls are to die, and with it, any hopes of your lineage's survival."

Before I could clapback, the girl she had been whispering to, threw herself overboard. The other three, who were still all tangled up, immediately felt the impact. The girls screamed and everyone attempted to pull her back up, but the ship lurched violently, and almost on cue, all the girls went over.

Horrified, I peered over the rail. I couldn't see anything. The

69

sun was setting, the water was dark and there were tears in my eyes. Everyone seemed to be holding their breath. We were all looking for some sign of life, but there was nothing. After an eternity, one of the white men started pushing everyone back to the lower level of the ship. I looked around and saw that the assassin was gone. She had completed her mission.

I wiped my eyes and prepared to jump back to the present. As I meditated on it, I heard a noise. It sounded like something was blowing water. Looking out at the ocean, I noticed a beautiful blue whale traveling away from the ship.

IV

Part Four

"The world is going to tear you down by default.
Whatever strength you can muster to survive, survive."

Journey To Ghana (Post-apocalypse)

My Maame was the fiercest warrior I had ever seen. She looked like she was dancing whenever she fought and her body seemed to move to drums I couldn't hear. Sometimes after a kill, I felt scared. Not because I thought she was going to hurt me, but because of how powerful she was. She was shorter than me, but beautiful with dark brown skin, a curvy body and a nearly bald head. She kept her hair short, because she claimed it made her look more intimidating. But I knew that the real reason was because, when she was seventeen, she almost died after her long locs got entangled during a fight with an akokromfi. She shaved her head the next day.

We were headed to the ocean. Last year, we had heard about a boat that took people to Ghana. There was a protected community in a small town outside of the city Obuasi where regs and *Blessed* lived peacefully. The boat only came once a year and only took the first 263 people. We had been traveling for seven months on foot. We had to make it to the coast of a place called North Carolina and we only had two more months to get there.

It was me, my sister, my uncle and my baby brother tied around Maame's back. As a group, we appeared weak when traveling, but all of us were trained in Donga, Nguni and various forms of stick fighting. Maame always instructed us to use our sticks first and only upon her say so. She was trained in everything from weaponry to martial arts to boxing, you name it! She had been training since she was two and did not play. With the baby on her back and only a rake for clearing away overgrown shrubbery, she always looked like she was at a disadvantage, but nothing about her was weak. I had seen her do a flip off a tree, kick a man in the head and stab him with her rake, all with my baby brother on her back. She always fought first and we were not allowed to fight unless she tagged us in. There had been many times where it looked as if Maame was losing, but she still refused to tag us in. She was afraid that if anyone found out about our fighting abilities, they would send word to others. Maame didn't want there to be a bounty on any of our heads. Her sole purpose of living was to protect us, and that was a task done regularly.

My ten-year-old sister Kisi specialized in crude weaponry and could wield all weapons with tremendous accuracy. She could make a weapon out of anything. I had once seen her take someone's eye out with a pinecone and a leaf. To this day, I still couldn't figure out how she did that. Kisi was already almost as tall as Maame and had brown skin with locs down to her shoulders. She often wore her bandanna around the top of her head.

Uncle Yokow was fourteen and specialized in hand-to-hand combat. He once took down a 250-pound man with a chop to the neck just by hitting the right pressure points. Uncle Yo was dark brown with the most beautiful skin I had ever seen. His tall, lanky body didn't seem to match his skills, but he made it work. Most recently, we had been attacked by a group of regs. The alpha male approached Uncle Yo first. Because he was tall for his age, sometimes, people assumed that he was older—let's just say we doubled our food and water supply that day. He wore his bandanna around his neck.

And I, Mawusi, was tall and light brown. I had just turned twelve and used a bandanna to wrap my braids up. I often brought the element of surprise to any situation. Sometimes, it worked for us and sometimes it did not.

There were many other groups as well, but each of us were just trying to find a way to survive the End. We had been attacked by many groups along the way. Sometimes, the groups wanted my Maame, sometimes the groups wanted Uncle Yo. Sometimes, the groups just wanted me and my sister.

I was exhausted from battle. We were currently in what used to be Texas and it had to be about 500 degrees. I hated this place and so did my armpits. We had been traveling for ten days straight, only stopping at night and for five-minute breaks throughout the day. We lucked up and came across a cornfield. Maame always said certain plants were resilient and would grow in any conditions and I guessed corn was one of those plants.

The corn field was taller than Uncle Yo and looked scary. Maame didn't trust the situation. She didn't trust anything, but especially not an empty field of corn. She only wanted to get enough to fill our sack and leave quickly. She was going to go into the field alone and gather corn while we hid in the brush. As always, she gave us instructions on what to do if she did not come back, we had heard this conversation a thousand times. We were not under any circumstances allowed to intervene if she got into a fight.

We watched Maame creep to the tall stalks and pick a bagful of white corn when we all felt it—something was about to go down. As she tied up her bag to throw over her shoulders, we heard a hissing noise coming from inside the corn stalks. Maame

75

had been careful to only pick corn on the edge of the field, not knowing if there was any danger lurking further. We heard the hissing again and knew that if we could hear it from our distance, Maame most definitely could. If the hissing was what we thought it was, she was in danger.

Uncle Yo remained still. He was always good at listening to Maame. Kisi, on the other hand, was fidgeting. She had built a new weapon the night before and was looking for a reason to use it. Uncle Yo was in charge by default because he was the oldest. With the baby tied around him, he crouched lower into the brush and gave us the quiet sign. Kisi rolled her eyes and crouched lower. I took one more glance at Maame, who was headed back from the cornfield and crouched down as well. I had just settled down into a comfortable position when we heard a voice call out. Swiftly, we looked towards the corn fields. Two ananses were still somewhat in their human form and Maame took the opportunity to take them out. Swiftly, she knocked the bigger one down. As she went for the second one, it started pleading in English. I knew what was going to happen next. She wouldn't be back for a while and would go off in a different direction for at least thirty minutes to make sure no one else was following behind.

I sat down in the brush and closed my eyes. The time went by quickly, and when I opened my eyes, Maame was standing over me. "Mawusi, you are never to fall asleep on a mission! You could have put your siblings and your uncle at risk."

I felt bad, we had made lots of mistakes since we started our journey some months before, and we had laid down some ground rules. "I'm sorry, Maame. I am tired and hungry. It's so hot here."

She touched my face softly and lowered her head to mine.

She pressed her forehead onto mine and then kissed it. "I understand Usi, and as long as we're alive, there's room for forgiveness." I loved her so much. When we made mistakes, she didn't beat us like other mothers I had seen; she scolded us, and then, loved us harder.

There was a safe camp set up a few miles north of our location, and we had to find it before dark. Before leaving a place called Oregon, my Uncle Hiroji had given us directions and safe words to all of the camps along the way. He was already in Ghana making preparations for us to come. We had to memorize ten safe words each. Most of the safe camps had an Adinkra symbol somewhere near it. These symbols showed us the safe camps leading to the boat. Most times we could find a symbol on a tree or a boulder, but sometimes, the symbols were in the most random places like a bush or a huge leaf. I was excited because we had been walking for two weeks since the last safe camp. I wanted to bathe and sleep without looking over my shoulder.

As we neared the camp, Maame touched one of her tattoos. She was for hire in many ways and was currently carrying five different people to safety within her tattoos. It was possible to shrink a person down and freeze them in a piece of jewelry or a tattoo, and Maame always froze people in tattoos because she felt it was the safest, since nobody could rip them off her skin. Most were floral shaped and it was impossible to tell the difference between them and her actual tattoos. She had considered carrying us the same way, but didn't want us to lose time. Whenever a person was frozen, they stayed the same age and didn't grow. If the host died, the frozen immediately popped out and it took some time for them to be able to move again. Maame was dropping off an elderly woman to her son at the community we were heading towards. It was her only face tattoo—a beautiful pink flower. I was going to miss it.

We must have been nearing the community, because, suddenly, the air felt different. We had to keep our eyes peeled. There were always creeps hanging around in hopes of getting in.

Almost on cue, a group of men came out from behind some bushes. "Nanyamka. Looking stunning as usual." The leader of this group had been after Maame for some time and refused to take no for an answer, which was the very reason he was in Maame's "creep" category.

"Jakoob, the day I give you agency over my body, may my children feed me to the crows." Looking visibly hurt, Jakoob signaled to his men. A big, dangerous-looking man stepped forth. Maame usually never let us fight first, but she knew there was no real threat as Jakoob never travelled with *Blessed*. He was way too arrogant and only kept regs around to feed his ego. Uncle Yo took a step forward and prepared to fight, but Maame stopped him with her hand and motioned for Kisi instead.

Jakoob's men started howling as soon as they saw my sister step up. While they laughed and joked about not wanting to hurt a little girl, Maame and Jakoob never broke eye contact. "How many men will you lose Jakoob? All of this for a date? For a night with me? You don't care about your men—anyone foolish enough to follow you deserves their fate!" Jakoob remained silent but signaled for his man to fight. The man suddenly looked nervous. With a thick British accent, he inquired if Kisi was a monster.

Uncle Yo chuckled. "All human, homie!"

In addition to Kisi's skill with weapons, she was incredibly fast. With great hesitation, the man lunged at Kisi. With two quick moves, she took out his knees with a rock-hammer device before jumping on his back and breaking his neck. We never ever fought to injure—only to kill.

Jakoob's men were shook. Another ran forward in an attempt to grab Kisi. He never even touched her. With precision and speed, she took his left eye out. Speed was just as important as skill. In most cases, Maame preferred for us to fight with sticks to avoid being touched, but made an exception because they were regs. Maame had always told us that, in battle, if you allowed your opponent to touch you, you were already dead.

Two other men stepped forth and Maame finally tapped me in. I camouflaged between them, stabbing one in the neck and the other in the lung. Neither would survive. One looked at Uncle Yo. "I thought you said she wasn't a monster?" Uncle Yo shook his head and pointed at Kisi. "Naw, I said *she* wasn't a monster!"

I was a monster—at least that's what the humans called me. So far all I could do was camouflage. An old woman once said that I had not even begun to tap into my power, but regs assumed that everyone who wasn't completely human, was a monster. In our world, monsters were those who didn't have a human form. I had a human form, but I was still too young to transition to my true form.

There was a hierarchy in the *Blessed* world, and so much discrimination. Those who couldn't transform into a reg used to have to hide in the shadows. That was partly what The Great War was about or at least why so many monsters were willing to fight. Honestly, there was little difference between *Blessed* and monsters. We are all *Blessed* and having a human form should not be a badge of honor.

There were five men to go and they were all running towards us. Maame tapped in Uncle Yo. He was scrawny but lethal. He took out two men with careful punches to their sides, and then their temples before breaking their necks. The last three attempted to run away, but we never left survivors.

Jakoob remained unmoved as Maame sighed. The only reason she hadn't killed him was because she couldn't. He was *Blessed* and couldn't be killed, but could be seriously injured. She had concluded several fights back that he enjoyed being hurt by her. It was the touching and intimacy he enjoyed, so now she refused to even touch him.

Maame looked annoyed as she walked past him. "My children are hungry and tired. I swear I cannot wait to find a way to kill you." As we all walked past him shaking our heads, Jakoob said the safe word and we all walked into the safe camp.

Stepping into the safe camp was like stepping into another world. Without the safeword, the camp was hidden. Powerful magic made camps safe and shielded us from the outside world. The camps were peaceful and felt more like a community. I still couldn't figure out if they were a different dimension altogether and the *Blessed* who created them wouldn't tell me. There was safety in secrecy. I was the reason our group was able to enter into *Blessed* communities, being that I was the only *Blessed* member of our family. Honestly though, Maame was so well loved by the *Blessed*, I felt certain they would have let her in without me.

Maame's rule when first entering a community was to wash and change into our clean outfit. We carried two outfits at all times. One was on our body, and the other was neatly rolled into our backpacks. Maame often wore a shirt with two famous rap artists from a place called Atlanta, who were said to have been one of the greatest rap duos ever. For traveling and fighting purposes, all of our outfits were comfortable and lightweight.

I was ready to head to the wash area until I saw storytime had just started. My Auntie Siola'a was performing the story and she was my favorite storyteller. *Blessed* from Tonga were one of the few groups who could create visuals when performing. Maame said it was similar to watching a movie, an activity people used to enjoy before the End. I had heard it a thousand times before, but every time it was told, Auntie always added something different in.

I had to hear this story. "Maame, may I please watch Auntie perform? I will wash after. I will help others wash as well." Maame gave me a serious scowl that broke into a smile. She gave me permission, then continued to the wash area with my baby brother. She walked past my Auntie and blew her a kiss. Auntie pretended to catch it and press it close to her heart.

I settled down with Kisi and Uncle Yo, and the story began. "Many years ago, the ultimate power originated in Africa, and from there, was distributed to each tribe." Even though I had heard this story many times, I still sat on the edge of my seat like I was hearing it for the first time. "A group of witches strayed far from home, and settled in a foreign land that would later be known as Europe. They built up. They built castles, and monuments, and beautiful structures, not realizing that they were moving further and further away from the power source, which was in the earth." This part of the story always confused me. *Did they not realize that the power was in the ground? Did they not care? Why leave the power source?* "Those who realized this, remained close to earth, refused to conform, and were cast out or killed. By the time the others realized what had happened, their power had waned, and they had grown weak. With each generation, the power grew more and more faint... and then, jealousy struck like a ferocious lightning rod. The witches became jealous of one another. When they passed as regs, they

81

had privilege, but in the realm of magic, they were considered some of the weakest beings. So, they decided to awaken beasts that were never supposed to be bothered. These beasts were meant to fight their battles, but the beasts could not be tamed."

As I watched Auntie create a story of the timeline of events, I tried my best to understand a word Maame taught us: "racism". It was confusing to me, because I had never known the impact of this word. By the time I had come about, the only hierarchy was between regs and *Blessed*. And then there was extreme hierarchy within the *Blessed*. I couldn't even imagine a time where regs hated each other simply for what shade their skin was. It was puzzling. The time period before the End seemed ridiculous and stressful, mainly due to the regs.

Auntie had created a miniature storm to symbolize the Great War. This part always made me angry. Many good regs and *Blessed* had died within that seven-year period. They managed to come together and fight off the beasts who were trying to take over the earth. The cold part was that most of the witches who had awakened the beasts to fight their battles were killed off early by the very beasts they had awakened. They were bitter that witches from other lineages had more power than them. They started a war based off of jealousy and racism, but didn't even live to see the devastation that they left behind.

I felt sadness. We were all still living in the remnants of The Great War. Maame was pushing so hard for the move to Ghana, because she wanted us to know what peace felt like. Part of my sadness came from not knowing what "peace" was. She had explained the word, but it seemed so farfetched, I couldn't even imagine it. Battle had become my normal. We had all heard that Ghana had the safest community, and so many of our loved ones were already there. Maame hated fighting every day, and hated us having to fight even more. She said it wasn't normal to have killed people by the age of twelve, but I didn't know any different. All I knew was that we needed to get to that boat. Each day put us closer to getting on the ship and Maame would kill anyone who got in the way.

Dinner was coming up soon, and I wanted to get a seat next to a girl I had met at another community. She was a reg, but she was cute and made my heart flutter.

"Usi! Usi!" I heard from behind me. *Damn.* A reg who always seemed to show up at every community, had found me. Uncle Yo said he had a crush on me, but I found him repulsive. I told him I would slit his throat if he touched me, and so far, he had been careful not to do so. Catching up to me, he attempted to block my path. I flipped him over on his back and held my knife to his neck. "What do you want?"

Struggling to catch his breath, he stared at me with his goofy blue eyes. With pale skin and dark brown hair, he was the ugliest reg I had ever seen in my life. "I just wanted you to know that your mom's wife is here." He had my attention.

Maame's wife was one of the only people I had ever seen her truly in love with. She was *Blessed*, and the prettiest woman in the world, outside of Maame. She had dark skin and long dark hair that went down her back. She had a hoop nose ring on a chain that connected to an earring.

Most of the time, she wore her sari with jeans or sweats. I ran to where he said she was. She had just finished with a client. "Usi! How are you daughter?" Maame Siya embraced me and sat me down next to her. I laid my head in her lap and fell asleep listening to her hum.

When I woke up, I was laying on a cot, and my dinner was beside me. I hadn't realized how tired I was. Stepping out of the shelter, the air was wet. It must have rained. The annoying reg had been waiting nearby and ran up to me. I didn't have the patience.

My English was decent, so I attempted to articulate my feelings. "Rodlin, correct? I am not interested in you. I am not interested in being your friend or future lover. Your presence annoys me, and nothing you can do could ever change that."

Maame had taught me to be direct when it came to situations like this. She was big on people respecting others' space and bodies. It might sound harsh, but direct was the best way to go. Maame told me there was a time when men controlled everything, including the bodies of women. I had never known that time.

Rodlin remained quiet while I spoke and respectfully waited for me to finish. "I won't always look like this. One day I will be big and strong and will catch your attention."

I rolled my eyes. "Highly unlikely." Rodlin sauntered off like a wounded pup and I took the opportunity to see who else had made it to the community.

Everyone had found their group. Kisi was surrounded by kids her age, and they were comparing weapons and such. Uncle Yo and some other boys were attempting to talk to a group of girls. Finally, Maame was sitting with a group of women and talking, while nursing my baby brother. I didn't often feel lonely, but I did on certain occasions like this. I didn't have a group that I automatically fit in with and I had a hard time talking to kids my age. Maame must have sensed how I was feeling, because she called me to come and sit with her and the other women.

I obliged, and for the next few hours the women gossiped, cried, laughed, and planned. I loved this time, and I loved how respected Maame was. Everyone loved hearing her stories of battle, and especially of the Great War. Maame was a good storyteller, but always acted as if she were not. One of the women switched gears and started talking about her trifling husband. Even with only the light from the fire, I saw the pain cross over Maame's face. She had not yet healed from my father.

Over a year ago, Maame had been attacked after gathering food and supplies. During the attack she was beaten and raped. She became pregnant with my brother and my father disappeared not long after. There was an attack at a trade town he was doing business in. It wasn't a safe guarded community, so we feared the worst. We continued our travels, and months later, Maame gave birth to my brother. It was one of the worst experiences of our lives. We were miles away from a community, Kisi, Uncle Yo and I had to deliver the baby. We all almost died that night, because we were attacked during the birth. Kisi saved all of our lives by one of her weapon inventions, but ever since, I was afraid of the baby. He wasn't like other babies and Maame was afraid he would not survive the journey. So far, he was still alive.

One day, we came across a community that had not been on our map. We were only able to get in, because we met someone else entering, and they took us with them. Stepping into that community felt eerie. Something was different. The people seemed like they were on drugs, even the children. We had barely washed for dinner when Maame spotted my father walking out of a shelter with his arms around two women.

Maame almost killed him. Her rake was to his throat, and anyone that came near, she put down. "We waited for you. We were nearly killed almost fifty times during this journey, and you have been here the entire time? Do you think I care about you being with another lover? I absolutely do not, but we missed you. Your children missed you. We almost died while I was giving birth."

My father who had been quiet up to this point raised his lowered head. "That is not my child. Why would I care if you almost died giving birth to that bastard?"

The crowd was quiet. Thoughtfully, Maame lowered her rake. "This is why you fled? I was raped. You know that—but any man who would abandon his wife after a sexual assault, while abandoning his actual children in the process, is no man I want to be with. If you didn't want to be with me, that is fine... but why did you leave your children?" Upon hearing that, he attempted to keep me and Kisi, but my mom threatened to murder him and the entire community. We left the next morning.

Listening to the women talk about their relationship woes, hurt her. I decided to switch gears. "Maame, have you seen Maame Siya?"

She smiled realizing what I had done. "Yes baby, and I will see her again after I put your brother to sleep."

I woke up later to hear Maame and Maame Siya arguing. I listened closely to what they were talking about. The sun had not yet come up, but based on how the birds were chirping, I could tell it was morning.

Maame Siya spoke Twi and they were having a heated discussion. "But why not let me transport the kids there? It would be easier on everyone. I could take two of them with me!" Maame was quiet. "Do you not trust me? Are they not my kids too?"

Maame moved closer. "I trust you. But I don't trust that method of travel. You have only tried to transport someone with you once and it ended badly." Maame Siya clicked her tongue and switched to Hindi. Maame was fluent in about nine languages and switched to Hindi as well. Listening to them go back and forth made me wonder about Maame Siya's travel ability. I was tired of walking and wouldn't mind volunteering to test out the method. I yawned and fell back to sleep.

I woke up to yelling. I slid on my pants and a sweatshirt, and ran out of the shelter. In the middle of the community, a man was crying. His husband was on the ground, not breathing. People had surrounded them, and everyone was trying to help. We needed a healer, and the only healer in the community had left the night before to gather roots for medicine near the mountains, a three-day journey at least. As everyone looked on helplessly, I saw Kisi standing close, too close. *What is she doing?*

Kneeling close to the man, she started to touch his legs, his arms, and his head. She had just started to touch his chest, when I attempted to grab her, but Uncle Yo stopped me. Something was going on. Kisi's eyes had turned all white and she looked different. She placed her little hands on his chest and pressed down hard. With two taps, she pulled something through his chest and into her hand. She turned to the crowd with her eyes still completely white. Opening her hand, we saw a yellow frog leg. "He will be ok, but you all should know that he was poisoned."

After getting over the initial shock, I went and found Maame. "Maame, did you see Kisi? She helped that guy!"

To my surprise, Maame didn't look happy at all. "Yes, Usi. I saw. Your sister is a healer."

I was confused at the sadness I was sensing. I assumed she would be thrilled that Kisi was *Blessed*. "Maame, why are you upset?"

With tears flowing down her cheeks, she hugged me tight. "Kisi no longer belongs to us—she belongs to the healers."

Most healers didn't fully come into their abilities until their twenties. The fact that Kisi was healing at ten, meant she was going to be exceptional. But she would need years of training and would have to leave us. She needed to be with her own kind. Maame was devastated. We waited until the healer came back from the mountains.

The woman was an elder, but did not look old. She was very kind and spoke gently to my Maame. "I understand how painful this is. In most situations, she would have been an adult by the time she started showing her talent. I can train her." Maame couldn't even speak. She nodded and kept wiping away tears. Kisi was joining another family, and there was nothing we could do to stop it.

The next few days were a blur. Maame used the time to give Kisi as many life lessons as possible. Kisi seemed dazed, and not herself. It was a lot for me to take in, so I could only imagine how she was handling it. We were a close family, and it hurt us deeply. We also hustled doing labor for the supplies we needed. Mom braided hair, Kisi cut hair, Uncle Yo gave fighting lessons, and I did nails and makeup. You wouldn't believe how many people still wanted to look beautiful in the midst of such awful circumstances. The day before we were supposed to leave, the elder healer came to our shelter.

Entering respectfully, she sat in front of my Maame. "I need to travel somewhere, and I heard you were the one to help me." Maame remained quiet. "I need to get on a ship headed home."

Maame stood up. "Where exactly do you need to go?"

The healer remained seated. "Ghana."

The healer would allow us to remain together, as long as we allowed her and another person to travel with us. Kisi would start her training immediately. I was ecstatic to still have my baby sister! Maame was happy, but weary. The healer refused to be frozen in a tattoo and her plus-one was a reg. I was anxious to meet who would be traveling with us.

While waiting for them to come to our shelter, Rodlin popped his head into our door. "Usi! Usi!"

I rolled my eyes. "If you're coming to say goodbye, good riddance!" Maame had taught us a bunch of terms and phrases that were used when she was little. Periodically, I liked to test them out.

Rodlin grinned his goofy grin. "I'm coming to say my bags are packed and I am ready to go!" *Shit.*

Maame and the healer were going back and forth. Maame was trying to explain to her that everyone who traveled with us could defend themselves. She was trying to remain respectful, but I could tell she was losing her patience. "Maame Brit, it is dangerous to have a reg, especially a child, traveling that cannot fight."

Hearing them go back and forth was tiring. The healer wouldn't allow Rodlin to be frozen either and assured us that he would be fine. *This is a circus!* I stepped out the shelter. I needed to walk and clear my mind.

I had barely gone five feet when Rodlin caught up to me. "Please, not now."

He slowed down. "I know you don't like me. And I know I get on your nerves, but I can defend myself. I have been defending myself for the last six months since my parents died. I am just grateful I will be in your presence."

Damn, I didn't know his parents had died. Come to think of it, I hadn't seen them at the last few communities. *Had he been with the healer this entire time?* "I'm sorry to hear about your parents, but I will still slit your throat if you touch me." With that, I walked to say goodbye to Maame Siya.

She was crying when I entered and I knew why. She hated leaving us. She could travel through space and time effortlessly and refused to make the walk with us. "Come here, daughter. You are getting so big and beautiful." We embraced. She unraveled my two long braids. Carefully, she washed, oiled, combed, and rebraided my hair. "Take care of your mom." She kissed me on the forehead and sent me on my way.

Maame had not yet found the son of the older woman she was supposed to be delivering and she would have to continue her travels with the flower face tattoo. This pleased me, and Maame pretended to scowl at my happiness. "Maame, it looks so beautiful on your face. I wish your entire face had flowers."

Sadness washed over Maame's face. I knew what memory I had triggered and felt bad. Seven years ago, Maame had met a Nhwiren in battle. Maame had gotten separated from us and was missing for seven days. During that time, she fought a Nhwiren and was almost killed. At some point, she and the Nhwiren made peace and mated. Shortly after, the Nhwiren disappeared. Somewhere she had a Nhwiren child, but no way to find it. They were a secretive type and could blend in with any plant environment.

A few communities ago, a Nhwiren had walked passed Maame and she almost fainted. She called out to the creature and ran up to it. It stood over nine feet tall and was covered entirely in flowers, vines, and other plants. There were flowers that seemed to bloom and close where the eyes should be. It was very expressive and unsettling. When she tried to inquire about her former lover, the Nhwiren didn't seem to understand and Maame walked away defeated. I knew the flowers were a painful reminder, but until the child was found, she never wanted to forget.

We said our goodbyes to the elders of the community and set out. We had only been traveling for two days when we came across a witch. Maame was cool with most witches and having a healer with us was almost an added bonus. Wearily, Maame asked the witch if she was sunshine in a meadow, an old trick people used to determine how safe the situation was.

The witch, who had been quiet up until this point, screamed "Run!" Within a matter of seconds, we were surrounded. There were regs and *Blessed* coming from the bushes and trees. Now we just had to see what the hell they wanted.

With every group there was always a leader. The leader was most often pompous, arrogant, and annoying in some way, usually a reg who had enough juice to convince the others to follow them. None of us had the patience. Every minute we wasted could be used to get closer to the boat. Also, what was the angle with the witch, and why was she being used as bait? A woman stepped forward, which worried me. Women leaders were especially vicious sometimes, because they felt they needed to prove a point and usually wanted to fight.

Maame stepped forward, preparing to deliver her script. Fighting was the last thing we wanted, so if we could, we always attempted friendly dialogue. "Me and my family are trying to pass through. We are headed to the boat and would appreciate safe passage." Maame lowered her head to add some humility to the situation.

"Raise your head, Nanyamka, and drop the act."

Maame lifted her head slowly and squinted. "Forgive me, but I do not know your name."

The woman stepped closer. "You wouldn't know it, because I am not important. Now, we both know you alone could level out all of my men. But would you be able to do it before I put a sword through that baby on your back?"

Maame was done with pleasantries. She stood up straight. "How about we find out?" She shifted into her fighting stance and I held my breath.

"I don't want to do this. I am not here to fight. I need someone that you are carrying. A man. Russian. In his twenties." I knew exactly which tattoo she was talking about. It was a mythical creature that wrapped around Maame's thigh.

"We both know that isn't going to happen. I was paid already and I intend to finish the job."

The woman shook her head. "You don't even know who you are carrying. That man is a monster. He has killed, pillaged and raped for centuries. He is an old war criminal, hiding in that young body."

Maame froze. I knew she was thinking about the "rape" part. She had so much healing to do. "I intend to deliver this man to his destination. I'm asking you one more time, let us pass."

Maame used to be an assassin for hire. She had been killing since she was fifteen and had gained quite a reputation. She always went in masked with her locs wrapped up high on her head. She had killed so many: preachers, lawyers, doctors, peasants, even children. The children were considered collateral if regs, and purposeful if *Blessed.* Maame only killed for a season and would disappear without a trace. If she ever had any regrets, it would be her time as an assassin. She was young and struggling to survive with baby Uncle Yo and assassin money was plentiful, allowing Maame to take care of him. His mother had died during his birth, so Maame was the only mom he had ever known. Their father had died the year before The Great War started, and Uncle Yo was born a few months before then. She treated him like she treated us. And he was more of a big brother than an uncle.

Maame was never one for a stare down. With swift precision, she hit the woman on her head with the handle of her rake. With one move, she took down the man nearest to her. In a blur, she flipped back and took down two more men. Not one person had been able to lay a hand on her yet, but she hadn't hit the woman hard enough. She stood quickly and put her knife to my neck.

Maame knew I was safe, but I could still see the anger flash across her face. She sighed. "I have already killed two of your men. I have no idea why you need this man, but I suggest you take your quarrels up with the handler. This right here—the fighting... the knife to my daughter's neck... the back and forth... it all leads to one road: your death."

Maame gave me the signal and I flipped the woman over and slit her neck. Taking out the rest of her crew was done with ease. Some of them put up a fight with special weapons or their *Blessed* abilities, but for the most part, it was an easy kill.

Walking over to the witch, Maame inquired what her role in this was, and almost instantly, the witch disappeared. Apparently, she had been set free once the woman was killed. *Convenient.* We checked to make sure everyone was ok and saw Uncle Yo had fallen by a tree, hit with an arrow that was stuck deep into his shoulder.

Maame and the healer started rummaging through their bags for supplies to help. I pressed my bandana around the wound to help stop the bleeding. While we were all tending to him in preparation of fixing the wound, Kisi leaned over him and her eyes turned white. She pressed both hands around the arrow, and within seconds, it popped out. Maame and the healer were speechless. Kisi formed a circle with her hands and put them around the wound, and we could see the tissue repairing itself before our very eyes. She never spoke a word but continued to keep the circle shape with her hands. Within ten minutes, the wound was completely closed. Then, Kisi sat back and fell asleep against the tree.

Maame and the healer spoke Xhosa to one another, a language I was not familiar with. She only did this when she didn't want anyone to hear the conversation. Waking up from her nap, Kisi interrupted, inquiring about something Maame had just said. Maame rolled her eyes. She had forgotten that Kisi as a healer and could now understand all languages.

Switching back to Twi, Maame questioned the event. "What does this mean? How can a healer heal a human?"

The healer just kept shaking her head slowly back and forth. "I don't know. I have never seen this in person, and I only heard legends of a healer who could heal both humans and *Blessed*. Either Yokow is also *Blessed*, or Kisi is surely going to be the greatest healer that ever walked the earth."

We took a few hours to rest and got back on our feet. We had barely entered Louisiana when we were slapped with a gust of wind that hit all of us so hard, it knocked us down. Maame must have understood what was going on, because worry began to creep across her face. Since the healer was the only other adult, they stepped to the side to whisper.

Rodlin took the opportunity to talk to me and I was instantly annoyed. "Usi, your fighting style has become quite advanced. Soon you will be a legend like your mom." It was no secret that my Maame was a living legend. Everywhere we went, there were stories about her. Some of the stories were true, some of them embellished, but most were entertaining.

I decided to be nice. We were going to be traveling together for a long time, and it actually was quite exhausting being mad at him all the time. "Rodlin, thank you." His goofy face lit up, and he attempted to come in for a hug. My knife was to his throat within seconds. I gently slid it across and a thin string of blood appeared. "That was a warning."

The healer walked over with Maame behind her. "The wind you felt a few minutes ago indicated that we stepped into another dimension." All of us looked around and at each other. It looked like the exact same landscape. *How could that be?* I had heard about different dimensions, but did not understand what it meant for us in this situation.

Maame could see the confusion on everyone's face. "Certain members of the *Blessed* safeguard their communities from outsiders with traps. That's why this community was not on the map. We must have stepped into their territory, and for their protection, they shipped us into another dimension."

Uncle Yo was perplexed. "How can they do that? Can't we just step back over? We crossed right over there."

The healer shook her head. "It's not that simple, child. It may look like the same landscape, but I can assure, we are very far away from our world."

Maame attempted to explain to us that we needed to find a clue as to how to leave. Every dimension had something that helped people figure out how to get back to their world. The problem was we didn't know the area well enough to know what belonged and what didn't. Some dimensions were so similar to others, that it could take years to spot a clue. As we walked around trying to find something, I got an eerie feeling we were being watched. I looked around at the town that was completely deserted, but I couldn't shake the feeling.

Kisi spotted a building that looked like an old timey bar with swinging doors. "Maybe we can find a clue in there." Before we could stop her, Kisi entered. Maame was quickly on her heels and had barely opened her mouth to scold her for being reckless, when a glass bottle flew off the shelf. Then, a mirror cracked completely in half, without anyone being near it.

Suddenly, a basket of peanuts went flying towards Maame's head. Ducking, her and the healer looked at each other. "Ghost dimension," they said together in perfect unison.

The *Blessed* who had sent us here were wicked. Ghosts were extremely dangerous, and if we were in a dimension of all ghosts, we were most likely going to die.

Maame had a plan. "Kisi, I'm going to do something that you aren't going to like. But we have to do it for our safety. I'm going to kill myself and you are going to bring me back." She explained that she was going to slice her throat to the point of near death and then attempt to navigate the dimension as a ghost. The plan was dangerous and had little chance of success with multiple ways to fail. *What if she dies before Kisi can bring her back? What if she got lost in the ghost dimension?* I didn't like this.

Kisi had her brave face on, but I knew she was terrified. We all were. Maame always talked about making wise decisions, even though she did things like this. There had to be another way. Voicing my concerns to her were useless. She already had her mind made up, and nothing we could say would change it. After giving quick instructions to Kisi and the healer, she gave us all a kiss and put the knife to her throat. Maame had slit hundreds, if not thousands, of throats. *What's one more?*

Maame's slice was clean and deep. Grabbing her throat, she fell back and Uncle Yo and I gently brought her to the ground. There was so much blood that seemed to be bubbling out of her throat. I felt sick and bit my lip to hold back tears. I tasted my own blood. Maame was close to death, I could feel it. She closed her eyes and died.

The next several minutes were terrifying. Not just because of Maame dying, but because of what was taking place in the room. Bottles were flying, glass was cracking, tables and chairs were being thrown and broken. Five minutes passed, and it was time to bring Maame back to life. I prayed this would work.

Kisi's eyes turned white and her little hands wrapped around Maame's neck. Within a few minutes, the slash in her throat was completely healed, but Maame wasn't waking up.

Eyes still white, Kisi looked up to the healer for guidance. "Place your hand on her chest and restart her heart." With uncertainty, Kisi place her hand on Maame's heart, but nothing happened. Kisi's eyes began to return to their regular color. *This isn't going to work.* I grabbed Kisi's hands, and with my hands over hers, I hit Maame's chest as hard as I could. Kisi sent a lightning bolt through Maame's chest and she jolted up.

Looking past all of us, Maame spoke. "I know how to get out of the ghost dimension."

With great detail, she explained what she had experienced in death. As a ghost, time was different, and she had actually been gone a few hours. When she first died, she was attacked by some cowboys who frequented the bar. She killed all of them—well, as much as someone could kill a ghost. Any death experienced in the ghost dimension was only temporary.

Maame had left the bar and walked down the street. She said the streets were busy and lively with people from different time periods. She saw women in big dresses, men in suits, rap artists from the early 2000s. She was actually enjoying herself. As she continued on, she met an old Japanese man who asked her to have tea with him. She agreed.

Stepping into a small space that looked like it might have been an occult shop, the man spoke to her in Japanese. "You don't belong here. And I can get you back to your dimension."

Maame was skeptical of all things and made sure he knew it. "At what cost? Nothing is free."

The elderly man chuckled. "You are certainly your father's daughter." As much as Maame wanted to take the bait and ask him what he knew about her father, she waited. "Your father was my pupil. I had gone to Ghana to see what all the fuss was about. The Chinese had started buying up land at an alarming rate, and some of my Japanese comrades sent me to Ghana to see if anything was worth investing in. None of that was my job or even my expertise. I was a martial arts instructor and knew nothing about real estate. They were trying to distract me because my wife had just died. They figured if I went to Ghana, I would at least be able to think about something else in a different environment. I met your father in a small village east of Accra. I walked up on him surrounded by older boys who were taunting him. The entire time your father never said a word. He just waited."

"What was he waiting for?" It was the first time Maame had spoken since he began his story and the elderly man squinted disapprovingly at the interruption.

"What do you think he was waiting for? For them to strike. Words mean nothing until a punch is thrown. The tallest of the boys walked in the middle of the circle to push your father, but he never even touched him. With a swiftness I had never seen in a child, he flipped the older boy on his back. I knew at that moment your father had to become my pupil. If I trained him, only for him to train the fiercest warrior that ever lived, then I did my job."

The Japanese man told her to find the grave of a witch that

lived long ago and to pick the flower that grew around her grave. The flower needed to be brewed into a tea and drank by everyone. As Maame was leaving, he warned her that things were not what they seemed, and to trust herself.

Maame explained that we were to stay together, and not to trust any illusion that appeared to us. We also needed to check every graveyard for the witch's grave. We were looking for a pretty plant called the Louisiana Phlox, a lavender wildflower that should still be in bloom and would be growing all around her grave.

The first graveyard was a bust. Not only did we not find the witch's grave, but some soul must have hated me, because they busted my lip. Kisi was able to heal it, but I still wanted to fight that ghost.

The second graveyard was the first time we actually saw a ghost. The healer explained that any of the ghosts could appear to us—they just needed to know how. A girl around six wearing an old-looking dress watched us check all the graves.

When I got to her grave, she appeared beside me. "This is your grave?" The little girl nodded. "You were only five years old. What happened to you?"

The healer came closer. "Usi, be careful. Like the old man said to your mom, things are not always what they appear to be." No sooner had the healer walked off, when the little girl grabbed my wrist. She had a tight grip and wouldn't let go. Before I could call for help, she sucked me into her grave.

I was expecting to be surrounded by dirt or something like that, but instead, I was sucked into a room that resembled a kitchen. There was an oven, refrigerator, and counters. There was also a table and two chairs, with a big-haired woman sitting in one of them. She was smoking a cigarette and blowing the smoke out obnoxiously. There was a sign above her head that read SOUTHERN GIRLS LIKE EVERYTHING BIG. I hadn't a clue what any of it meant, but I was grateful Maame had taught us how to read and write in English. I was nervous and wanted to assess the situation as quickly as possible, but I was confused. I was clearly not in the graveyard anymore. *Was I still in the same dimension?*

The woman watched as I tried to figure things out, so I decided to question her. "The little girl... was that a trick to get me close to the grave?"

The woman smiled. "No, she is very much a real ghost."

I stood up and wiped the dirt from my clothes. Normally I wouldn't be so disrespectful as to dirty a person's floor, but I could tell this entire situation was going to get ugly. "What do you want? How do I get back to my family?"

In a thick southern accent, she went into her story. The woman had been working as a secretary in a well-known law office. She worked in a small town, so everyone knew everything about everyone. She started having an affair with one of the lawyers in the office. She said that his wife walked in on her, and the next thing she knew, she was in this room.

I observed the woman. I should have felt sorry for her, but my survival was my top priority, and I still needed to get out of this room. "So, where does the little girl come in? Does she do your bidding?"

The woman chuckled. "No. She does that all on her own. She has her own backstory."

I shook my head. "But that doesn't make sense. She sucked me into her grave. How did I end up with you?"

The woman giggled. "Sweetheart, you're in ghost town. Nothing makes sense."

This was a lot. My head started to hurt. I wanted Maame. "You still haven't told me what you want with me, or how I get out of here."

The woman shrugged. "I have no idea how you get out of here. But when you do... I need you to deliver a message. That lawyer I was talking about? He is still alive in my dimension. Deliver him this message, and I might be able to summon the little girl."

She wasn't making sense. At first, she said she did not know how I could get out—now she was saying she could help if I delivered a message. She was purposely being confusing, and it was too much for me. For the first time, the woman stood up and began to walk towards me. She looked much scarier standing up than when she was sitting down.

"Hurry, child. Decide quickly. Will you deliver the message or not?" Her face had changed. In just a short amount of time, she looked like she had aged. Her voice also sounded different. Deeper. Scarier. My heart sped up. She was within arm's length and I was backed against the wall with nowhere to go. I was terrified. I screamed for Maame. Within seconds, a hand came from the ceiling of the room covered in dirt. On the thumb of the left hand was a monarch butterfly tattoo. It was Maame's.

I grabbed the hand. I knew she wouldn't be able to pull me up, so I pulled her down. The woman attempted to grab me and I kicked her across the room. I had successfully pulled Maame's upper half through, but her right hand was stuck on something. The woman had recovered from my kick and attempted to grab me again. With a hard tug, I pulled Maame's right hand through. In it was the little girl's head.

Maame slid the rest of her body through the ceiling, flipped, and landed on her feet like a dancer. "I don't have the patience for whatever you have going on here, but we have people up top prepared to burn your grave." The woman's face was in shock. The hole in the ceiling had completely closed up and the room had gone back to normal. The woman who had transformed into an older woman with decaying skin.

"You are clever. No one has ever been able to come through, who I hadn't sucked in myself. Smart girl. Now you both shall perish!"

Maame was still holding the head of the little girl. With one smooth motion, she lit it on fire with a lighter from her pocket. The old woman laughed as nothing happened. The little girl must have been a decoy to lure people into the grave. Maame dropped the head and took a step forward. It was time to fight.

Preferably, Maame would have liked to fight with her rake. There were *Blessed* whose very skin was their power and being touched by them could be deadly. Maame always made hand to hand combat her last option, but her rake must have been up top.

She punched the old woman in the face, but she just cackled. "You're no warrior, you're just a little girl." The old woman started to laugh hysterically as she turned Maame into a ten-year-old version of herself, revealing herself as a witch. I had suspected as much, but now I was certain. There was no way either of us could fight a witch, especially a ghost witch. *What the hell were we going to do?* The witch cackled and fell all over herself with laughter. "Maame, are you still in there?"

Little Maame looked so confused. She scanned the room before turning towards me. "I'm not sure what's going on, but I assume we are in trouble... and she's the threat?" I nodded. Little Maame lunged at the witch. Big Maame was terrifying, but she had nothing on the little girl version of herself. She was less disciplined, but she was amazing. With tiny flying fists, Little

Maame beat the witch's ass, tripping her before flipping her onto her back. She reached into her locs, pulled out a knife, and slit the witch's throat as I watched in awe.

I quickly reached into my backpack and grabbed the salt, pouring half the bag onto the witch's wound. She would come back eventually, but it bought us some time. Hopefully by the time she woke up, we would already be gone.

With the witch's death, came the release of all the souls she had tortured. Maame transformed back into her adult self and the little girl ghost stood before us. She said no words, but her eyes told us she was thankful. She turned to walk into the wall, but I stopped her to ask where the exit was. She looked towards the ceiling and then disappeared. As quickly as possible, we stacked the table and chairs on top of each other, creating a crude ladder to the ceiling. Maame pushed against the ceiling and was able to put her hand clean through. Without a second thought, she pushed me through the ceiling as hard as she could.

I felt like I was breathing for the first time. It was nighttime, and I could see the stars. Uncle Yo and Kisi pulled me through. Maame was pulled through seconds later. Standing up straight, she wiped away the dirt from her clothes before pouring the remainder of the salt onto the grave and setting it on fire. The witch probably had access to many graves, but at least she couldn't use the little girl's ghost anymore.

We hadn't expected to remain there overnight and needed to set up camp for the night, but the healer said we needed to find the flower before we went to sleep. There were two more cemeteries within our view, and we were praying one of them had the flower.

The first one was huge. It would take us forever to search each grave and I was already exhausted. The old man said the witch's grave would have flowers growing everywhere, but this graveyard didn't have any that looked like that. *What a waste of two hours.*

The last cemetery was small, and it didn't take us long to find the grave or the witch. She was sitting in front of her grave, boiling something. "Took you long enough," she said simply. Her accent was one that I had never heard. She had smooth, light brown skin with hazel eyes. Her hair was wrapped in a colorful scarf and she wore a flowing white dress. Even with just the light from our flashlights, I could tell she was beautiful. "Your flashlights won't be necessary." Within seconds, the entire cemetery was lit up. I couldn't see where the light was coming from, and I honestly didn't care. We all finally decided to relax and put our backpacks down. "You all are safe here, and you can rest. I have prepared the tea from the flowers around my grave."

Maame was still on alert. As her jaw was clenched, I could tell that she hadn't yet let her guard down. "At what cost? We come here and not only have you prepared the tea, but you expect us to drink it?" Maame was speaking a language I was unfamiliar with. Kisi translated for us and told us they were speaking French.

"Awe, Nanyamka. You are as intelligent as you are beautiful. You have every right to be skeptical, considering your run in with Oda. She is a nasty witch indeed. But you are correct—there is a cost."

Maame took the baby off her back and gave him to Uncle Yo. "What do you want?"

The witch stopped stirring the tea and looked at Maame with piercing eyes. "Freedom."

In twelve years of living, I had experienced some horrific things. I had killed and had almost been killed. I had heard historical accounts of things that humans had done to one another, things that I could not understand. Even with that, nothing could have prepared me for the sadness that came from the witch's story.

During a time period called American slavery, white regs kept black regs hostage and forced them to do hard labor. The witch had been enslaved on a plantation here in Louisiana. She worked as a house slave her entire life and was the mistress's personal servant. She had been raped almost daily and forced to have her rapist's children. She was forced to work for seventy years before she transitioned into her *Blessed* form. She had been sold away from her family at a young age, so she had no one around to help her with the transition. Sometimes during one's transition, they can appear dead or like they weren't breathing, so they assumed she had died. A funeral was prepared for her and she was buried. The mistress came and put flowers on her grave, but the flowers were eternal flowers that locked the witch into a catatonic state. Unwittingly, the mistress had paused the witch's transition. The flowers that grew around her grave were actually a prison.

"So, you're not actually dead?" Maame asked. "I don't see how we can help you. And why should we trust anything coming from your mouth? For all we know, you were locked in your grave for a reason and letting you out could cause havoc."

The witch studied Maame and responded thoughtfully. "How much more havoc could I release on this world that isn't already in motion? Just check my body. If you find me to still be breathing, then you will know that I was telling you the truth." Maame hesitated. She looked at all of us, grabbed a shovel, and started digging. It took us an hour, but we finally dug down to the witch's coffin. It was old, but still in fairly good condition. We opened it. The witch was in an elderly form, but had not yet decayed.

The healer laid her hands on her chest. "There is a heartbeat."

The witch explained that when we left the ghost dimension, we needed to clear all the flowers away from her grave and burn the lavender leaves. As the adults went over the plan, I noticed scribble on the bottom right of the outside of the coffin and motioned for everyone to gather around. It looked like a bird with a broken wing.

The witch looked astonished. "This whole time I thought the mistress didn't know what she was doing, that she was putting the flowers around my grave because she cared. But she was purposely enclosing me in a tomb. But why? Do you think she knew about me? Maybe she found out about the hoodoo I was doing with the field hands? What could it have been?"

The healer and Maame tried to comfort her. "I wasn't alive during that time, so I only have slave narratives and such to go off of... but it's hard to imagine that anyone who would keep another person hostage because they were too lazy to do their own work, could be compassionate... and that goes for anyone associated with them as well. It's no secret that slave mistresses were often as vicious, if not more vicious, than the slave masters themselves."

The witch was devastated. "I served her faithfully until the day I couldn't. I nursed her kids, changed her rags, fed her... I just don't understand why? I honestly don't know how I would've ever gotten out. Everything I've learned has been from the ghosts of other witches here. None told me about this carving. Obviously, it played a part in keeping me imprisoned."

"Maybe not. Witches all have emblems or symbols they can connect with or that are part of their circle. If we figure out what the symbol on the bottom of the coffin meant, maybe we could free you. Let's start with the tea, I'm ready to be out of this dimension."

Before drinking the tea, we checked to see if any headstones had the symbol. None of none them had it, but we realized the symbol could have been on the coffin, much like the witch's. If the mistress had imprisoned anyone else, there was little way of knowing. We would just have to drink the tea and hope to be helpful from our own dimension.

* * *

Birds were chirping and my throat was dry. I rolled over and saw Rodlin too damn close to me. I sat up and saw that we had fallen asleep exactly where we had drunk the tea. The air felt different. We were no longer in the ghost dimension. I woke everyone up and walked to the witch's grave. We would have to dig her up again. I started pulling the flowers off her grave as Kisi joined in. Pretty soon, we had pulled off at least a hundred flowers. I slid a few flowers into my backpack while no one was looking as Rodlin, Uncle Yo and the healer started digging up the grave. While they were digging, Maame gathered all the flowers and made a small fire. We all covered our faces. We didn't know the strength of this flower and could not risk be being bounced into another dimension.

It seemed to take forever, but once the grave was finally dug, the healer advised that we cut the binding symbol from the coffin and throw it into the fire as well. It was a fool's technique of getting rid of a bind or curse, but sometimes it worked. When the fire had burned everything, we opened the coffin. The witch's elderly form was gone and she looked the same as when she had served us tea. Maame explained that it was common after a transition for a witch to take a more youthful form, and this witch appeared to be closer to Maame's age.

The witch looked like she was sleeping and I reached down to touched her hand. "No Usi!" Maame reprimanded. "We don't know what type of witch she is... for all we know her skin is the source of her powers. It could be deadly to us!"

As Maame scolded me, I felt the witch's hand move under mine. "Maame, she moved!" We all gathered around as the witch slowly opened her eyes and smiled. We had all been holding our breath, and let out a collective sigh of relief.

The witch traveled all throughout Louisiana with us and told us many stories along the way. One was about a field slave who rebelled and was killed for it. She had joined with brothers and sisters from other plantations and had planned to wage war against their oppressors. The witch's eyes misted up when telling the story. She had a fairly comfortable life in comparison to others and recalled being afraid to mess things up. As a house slave, her hands were soft, her clothes were cleaner, her food was adequate and she didn't have to deal with harsh weather conditions. She hung her head in shame. "I never worked the field a day in my life, and at one point, I wore that badge honorably. But now... I am disgusted with myself."

I went to hug her, but Maame stopped me. "Let her sit in this feeling. Our ancestors who worked the fields deserve for her to sit in this feeling." Eventually, the witch wiped her eyes, and we continued on.

We had just crossed the border into Mississippi when the witch fell backwards. She stood and attempted to cross with us again, only to fall down to the ground a second time. She got up, wiped the dirt from her dress and smiled at us tearfully. "It appears that I am a prisoner to Louisiana. This is where we part ways. I need to find the grave of my mistress and burn it! I will catch up with you all before you get to that boat." We all hugged the witch and watched as she made her way back into the woods of Louisiana. I hoped we would see her again.

* * *

Mississippi and Alabama were fairly uneventful. We fought here and there, but nothing interesting happened. Georgia was an entirely different story. We made it to a city called Macon. Besides the lack of electricity, it looked like what I imagined a real city would look like. People were bustling around, walking the streets, and acting like it wasn't the End. It was both scary and confusing.

I looked to Maame for guidance, but she simply put her hand over my mouth. The healer and Maame mouthed for us all to be quiet, and tip-toe around the people. *Ok, we're in danger—that makes more sense.* They led us into the woods, and away from the people, making sure not to interact with any of them. We walked for almost an hour, and it felt like I had been holding my breath the entire time. At one point, a man on a bike almost knocked me down, forcing me to fall backwards. Luckily, Maame caught me and covered my mouth with a single motion.

We were almost out of the city when the baby sneezed. The people, who had been loud and talkative the entire time, suddenly went completely quiet. In fact, *everything* went completely quiet. Every head turned and looked at us. All of their eyes turned silver. Maame didn't have time to give the baby to Uncle Yo. She shoved the baby at me and yelled for us to run! I began to sprint and looked back to see the people had Maame surrounded. I stopped in my tracks and yelled for Kisi to take the baby and keep going as I ran back for Maame.

Maame has many stories from The Great War. I had heard people tell stories about her that I knew were not accurate. One was when she had slayed a great beast that had risen from a cave. The beast was apparently the size of a building and had teeth as large as a full-grown human. It was massive. The story goes that Maame walked up to the great beast and slid a sword under its belly, gutting it. The beast died instantly. Maame told us it was only the size of a large truck, and that she defeated the beast was by poking it in the eye with the end of her rake. She pushed the rake in so far, she hit its brain. Sometimes, I thought of Maame's tales told by others and chuckled. As tactical as Maame was, her best fighting came from pure adrenaline and the will to survive.

I camouflaged my way through the crowd that was gaining on her. I put my back against hers and she turned to face me. "Usi, you must flee. Now!"

I shook my head. "I'm staying right here!"

I had never directly disobeyed my mother, and vowed that I never would again.

With tears in her eyes, she touched her forehead to mine. She kissed me and said a single word. "Survive."

The main reason Maame wanted to be the only fighter was because she didn't want to have to watch our back during battle. She fought better when she knew we were safe. This time, she would be looking over her shoulder and I would have to hold my own.

The first pair of silver eyes jumped at me and I took him out easily. The next six were just as easy. Around the ninth person, I felt my right arm beginning to hurt and switched to the left. Fighting with my left hand wasn't difficult, but I didn't have the same familiarity. Not long after, I started to notice that the people weren't actually fighting back—they were trying to grab us. None of them were warriors, they just had strength in numbers.

"Maame! Do you notice anything unusual?"

"This is not the best time, daughter," she said, slicing open two faces at once.

I couldn't shake the feeling. "What if they aren't trying to kill us?"

Maame clicked her teeth, and drove her rake into someone's chest. "I suspected that ten people ago, but they are still trying to capture us."

I don't like this. Something is off. "But what if they are being controlled or something—should we still kill them even if they don't know what they are doing?"

Maame was backed against a tree. "Usi, my love... even if they are being controlled, they are still causing us harm. They didn't greet us with bubbles and butterflies." I wanted to ponder more about she meant by "bubbles and butterflies," but the situation grew weirder.

Suddenly, all of the silver-eyed people stopped coming at us. Their hands and heads dropped, and they stood still. Maame didn't wait for an invitation to leave. She grabbed my hand and we started running. I looked back at the people, and could have sworn I saw a silver-eyed little boy peeking out from behind a tree.

It took us three hours to catch up with the group. They had entered a safe camp and joined the community. We all went our separate ways to bathe and prepare for dinner. My right arm was still aching and I wondered if Kisi could be of some help. I had never fought for such a long period of time and my body was sore. My mind kept thinking back to the child with silver eyes. People often thought of *Blessed* as those who transformed into monsters or animals, but forgot they came in all shapes and forms with endless types of abilities. Some could move buildings with their minds, while others could grow fangs.

I wanted to bring it up to Maame, but she was focused on dropping off three people with their family members, leaving her with three tattoos to go, including the rapist wrapped around her thigh. I shivered at the thought. I wished for her to take him off her skin, but she had a job to do. We stayed at the community for a shorter time than usual because we needed to get back on the road quickly. Most of the people we usually saw at the community were gone, meaning they were a few days ahead and closer to the boat. We needed to hurry up.

We got back on the road, and entered South Carolina within days with little trouble. It was similar to Georgia in terms of landscape, but the air was a little different. We were traveling to meet up with the Gullah people. For the first time in a long time, I was excited. I had heard stories that they were one of the few groups of regs who fought the beasts off without any help from *Blessed* during The Great War. Maame always scolded me when I talked about it. She was big on history, and always wanted us to note how amazing they were outside of the war. The Gullah people were one of the few groups of Africans living in America who had successfully maintained much of their West African heritage and customs.

The place we were going was not on any map. It was on the coast and we would need permission to enter. An elder man met us at the foot of the forest. *How did he know we would be here?* He never said a word, he simply turned around and started walking. We followed him through the forest in silence for a long time.

I checked my watch and saw that it had been an hour. As we continued to walk, I started to daydream about the day I got my watch.

Three years earlier, we had discovered a warehouse that had not yet been looted. It had been a distribution center for a well-known superstore, that was hidden by a thick forest, and couldn't be seen from the road. We didn't find any food, but found loads of clothing and supplies. Maame said we could get whatever we wanted as long as we were able to still carry our backpack. We stocked up on all the essentials: underwear, bras, flashlights, bugspray. I looked down at my watch with a smile. It was my most favorite thing.

It was almost entirely dark as the elder man took us deep into the woods. "Have you heard about that Bruh Rabbit?" he asked. He told us a story about an incredibly smart rabbit who was a trickster that got out of a lot of situations with his wit.

As soon as the elder man finished the story, the forest opened up with a woman standing at the edge. "No hags or haunts?" The elder man shook his head no.

I looked at Maame, but Kisi responded. "They wanted to make sure we didn't have any evil spirits attached to us." *So, Kisi could understand different dialects and slang too? Cool.* I began to wonder how the elder man was able to determine if we had anything attached to us when all he did was walk with us and tell a story.

The woman must have sensed my curiosity, because she came to walk beside me. "The forest you walked in is the forest of truth. The story you were told involved truth and lies. If you had any haunts on you, they would have come forth." I wanted to inquire more about the forest, but the brush opened up into a community. There were a few people by the water and a long walking-bridge that took us to a small island where everyone was.

I had never been to Africa, but I imagined this was what it looked like. There were brown faces everywhere. The women had babies tied on their backs, and baskets on their heads. Kids were running around the women and the men were carrying supplies to different places. The dwellings were similar to some of the huts I had seen in books about Africa. Maame had always reminded me that before the End, Africa had all types of buildings, just like the United States. There were mansions, skyscrapers, and hospitals. She also made sure I understood that a mansion was no better than a hut—that both dwellings served a purpose.

The Gullah welcomed us with open arms. Maame immediately went into a dwelling to take off one of her tattoos, remaining inside for over an hour. While she was gone, we washed and ate dinner. While waiting for her to come back, I had dozed off, only waking when I heard a baby cry out. I didn't pay it much attention, assuming it was my baby brother, even though he barely cried. Surprisingly, Maame emerged from the dwelling with a different baby instead. I looked at all of her tattoos and saw that the moon from her left arm was missing. *Why hadn't I known it was a baby she was carrying?* A woman rushed forward and fell on her knees. In Geechee, the woman cried and praised Maame as the entire village crowded around us.

When the excitement died down, the woman gently took the baby, and in English, asked if she had suffered. *If who had suffered?* I hated not knowing what was going on, but I knew better than to interrupt such an important moment. Maame shook her head. "No. But you should know that she died in a *Blessed* form."

The woman's eyes widened. "But we aren't *Blessed*. None of us are!"

Maame touched the woman's arm gently. "But your daughter was—in fact, she was very dangerous. That is why I had to kill her."

While listening to Maame, I started to remember the night the woman's daughter had died. We had seen her transform into her *Blessed* state and start killing those around her. I had never seen her species before and she was terrifying. She was over ten feet tall with spikes all over her body. I was so scared that I actually hid behind Maame. In fact, we all did. The creature kept circling a crying baby, not allowing anyone to get near.

Maame slowly gave my baby brother to Uncle Yo and approached the creature cautiously. "The baby, she is yours?" The creature hissed at Maame as a warning. "You have already killed five people. I will not allow you to kill anymore." The creature stopped pacing and eyed Maame. She understood. "You are now a part of the *Blessed*. Listen to me. Listen to my voice." The creature kept hissing and growling at Maame, unable to calm down. "If you can transform back to your human form, I will help you find your kind. I will not kill you, but I cannot allow you to kill anyone else. Hiss twice if you understand me?"

At the time, I almost laughed. I knew Maame didn't mean to make a joke, but I found it hilarious. Uncle Yo sensed my amusement and he looked at me with a shake of his head. The creature kept pacing around the baby as Maame continued to speak to her soothingly. Slowly, the pacing became less intense. Her growls ceased and she began to relax. The creature seemed to be able to follow Maame's voice. We were finally making progress.

Just as her eyes started to look more human, a man came out of the brush with a spear. He attempted to ram it into the creature but didn't even penetrate her skin. Within seconds, the creature had the man in the air with one of her spikes, ripping his head off with little effort. Another man ran towards her and Maame knew it was over. Any progress she had made up to that point would be undone because the men kept attacking the creature.

Despite this, Maame tried one last time to appeal to her. She looked at Maame, and charged at Kisi in desperation. Without hesitation, Maame slid her rake across the creature's throat, knowing she wanted to die. With dark blood bubbling out her neck, she only said one word. "Gullah." The older woman wept. Hearing how her daughter died hadn't made it any easier to deal with. Maame sat with the woman for hours and comforted her while nursing her granddaughter.

I took the opportunity to explore. Everyone seemed to be doing something. I was enjoying just walking and watching. A group of women were basket weaving and I sat down to watch. An older woman shook her head, and in Geechee, told me I needed to join in. I was not good with my hands like Kisi, but I picked up what looked like straw. The woman showed me how to weave the pieces together. I kept messing up, but eventually I got the hang of it. The women were so patient with me and my clumsiness.

When we were done, I was sad that it had come to an end and hadn't even noticed that it had become dark or that I was starving. We all sat down to eat in front of huge pit, and inside the pit, was a huge black pot. Whatever was inside smelled delicious. The bowls were passed around, and when mine finally came to me, I looked at it and picked up a piece of food with my fork. *What is this?*

Maame saw my confusion. "Shrimp. You have never had it, because we have never lived by water. This is called gumbo.

Don't be rude—take a bite." I sniffed it and took a bite. It was delicious. Before I knew it, I had eaten too much and Maame was helping me to my sleeping mat. "Yes, Usi, good food will give you the itis," she said with a smile. I floated off to sleep and dreamed of this "itis."

I had only been asleep a short while when I heard screaming. I had barely put the leg of my pants on, when I ran out of the dwelling. Maame had her rake at an older boy's throat.

The mother of the *Blessed* Maame had killed was on her knees begging her. My eyes were still sleepy, and though I kept rubbing them, I couldn't see clearly. "Please!" she begged. "He is just a boy, grieving his older sister! He didn't mean anything by it. He is still learning to control his anger!" The woman pleaded as Maame turned her head slowly, and I saw the blood trickling down her temple. There was no way he had fought her fairly. *He must have gotten the drop on her. Sneaky shit.*

I camouflaged my way closer to what was happening, and was barely within arm's length of the boy when he grabbed at me, causing me to jump back instinctively. *There was no way he could see me.* I had gotten good at camouflaging and I should have been invisible.

"I can see your heat signature," he said. "It's low, but it's there. Reveal yourself!"

Slowly, I uncamouflaged and stared at him. "You... you're one of us."

By now, the entire village had gathered around. The older boy looked to his mother who only shook her head and wept. He turned back to my Maame. "You killed my sister, and now you dare seek refuge in our village? You dare eat from our pot?!"

The older boy lunged at Maame, and she knocked him out with the end of her rake before glancing at his mother. "This is going

117

to cause issues. We will leave tonight."

We had had to leave in a rush before, but never like this. The boy wasn't a formidable enough opponent to run from. I liked the village and wanted to stay an extra day. Rodlin had also been exceptionally annoying, and I didn't feel like traveling beside him. I packed my bag angrily. I started to roll my cot, when I got an eerie feeling that I was being watched. I camouflaged myself and turned around quickly.

The older boy was standing in the doorway, with a huge lump on his head. "I can see you. Or at least the heat from your body."

I uncamouflaged and rolled my eyes. "What the hell do you want?"

He came and sat down on my cot, which annoyed me even more, because I would have to re-roll it. "I need you to get your mom to take me with her."

I looked him sternly in the face, going over every inch of his face with my eyes before busting out laughing. He sat unmoved, waiting until I finished. *Oh... he's serious.* "You just attacked Maame. I'm not helping you with shit."

He sighed. "How would you feel if your only sibling was killed, and the person who killed her marched into your village, received a dwelling, food and clothing?"

I thought about it for a minute and felt a pang in my heart at the thought of losing any of my siblings. "But that's not what happened and you know it. Your sister transitioned and didn't know how to control her powers. She killed more than five people. Maame pleaded with her to try and help. And then, your sister tried to kill my sister."

He shook his head and put his head down. "Did she... did she suffer?" I shook my head. "Will you just talk to your mom please?" After watching the older boy storm out of the dwelling,

I decided to talk to Maame, but I already knew what the answer would be.

"Absolutely not!" The boy's mother had gotten to Maame before I had and she responded exactly how I suspected she would.

The woman looked desperate. "Please. We have never had a *Blessed* living amongst us. He might not be taken well by others. If you take him with you, I can meet you all there when the next boat comes.

"I hear you. Every word. But your son struck me in anger. He will undoubtedly try to kill me the next chance he gets and he will not have you there to stop me from slicing his throat. Then, you will have two children dead by my hand."

The woman saw she wouldn't be able to persuade Maame differently. "Look at me. Look at my hands. This is over forty years of basket weaving. My health is decent, but I am in no condition to raise a baby *and* stress about my son."

Maame looked at the women's gnarled fingers and took pity on her. "There is a group coming in a few days. They can take him, but they will be traveling northwest, and will likely miss your village. Someone will have to meet them, but I can write a letter on his behalf. That's the best I can do, because he cannot travel with us."

We set out at sunrise. We had walked for at least three hours already, and I was still grumpy we had to leave early. Rodlin wasn't making things any easier either by being as annoying as possible. The baby was fussy, Kisi was doing her daily lesson with the healer, and Uncle Yo was in his own world. South Carolina also had some ridiculously big mosquitos.

Everything was making me angry and Maame must have felt it. "Usi, can you camouflage and climb those trees? I need to see how far from the water we are and I want to keep following the coastline to North Carolina." I knew she was giving me a task to keep my mind busy, so I obeyed.

The trees she asked me to climb were a little further back as we had passed them five minutes ago. *Glad everyone else gets to rest, while I climb these goofy trees.* Even through my grumpiness, I was still aware of everything around me and began to have an eerie feeling like I was being watched. My family was only a short distance away, so I knew if I yelled, they could come quickly, but the hair on the back of my neck was still standing up. I kept looking around, but I didn't see anyone and started to climb.

I was halfway up when I saw something move below me. I stopped climbing. I was camouflaged and should've been invisible. I saw movement again and looked down quickly, but still saw nothing. I was starting to feel completely creeped out. I wanted to call out to Maame, but didn't want reveal my location. I decided to finish my task. I got to the top and saw the water was just past the trees. I looked down quickly again, but still saw nothing.

I saw that I was close enough to jump to a branch on another tree and hopped over effortlessly. *Ok, I can do this.* I looked down and noticed that the tree didn't have enough little branches to step down. There were just two branches below me and they were quite a distance away from each other.

I jumped to the first branch, but the second branch was so far down. I attempted to see if my left leg could touch it, while still holding onto the other branch, but I couldn't. I told myself I would just have to fall and hope that I landed on the last branch, but the ground was too far down to attempt it. I was scared, but I knew my family was waiting. I took a breath and jumped.

I missed the branch and hit my shoulder on the tree trunk. I realized I was going to hit the ground and closed my eyes to brace myself for the fall.

Several moments passed and I realized I hadn't hit the ground yet. I opened my eyes and saw the head of a giant snake inches from my face. I let out a loud scream and fainted.

* * *

When I came to, Maame was rubbing my face with a cloth. I sat up and saw everyone was crowded around me. My eyes finally cleared and I noticed a new face. *The older boy from the Gullah village? Why is he here?*

I looked to Maame for an explanation, but she was too busy chastising him. "You need to go back home! Does your mother even know you ran off?"

The older boy puffed his chest out. "If I hadn't shown up, your daughter would have a broken neck! At least give me a chance. I promise I won't be any trouble! Just give me a chance!"

Maame shook her head. "No. You have a three-hour walk back home—you'd better get started."

The older boy would not let up. "I know I messed up. I was hurting. I'm still hurting... maybe your healer can help me. But I'm powerful and I know I could help this group."

The healer put her hand on his head and gave Maame a nod. "We don't have time for healing," Maame said sternly. "You can travel with us for now. At the first sign of anything wrong, I'm killing you."

The older boy put his hand out to shake on it. "My name is Malcolm."

* * *

We traveled up the coastline for what seemed like hours. Sometimes it could be hard for people who aren't used to walking long distances, so I kept glancing at Malcolm. He was quiet, but kept up with the rest of us. I still couldn't believe that he was the giant snake I saw before I passed out. I shivered. Snakes were creepy. He kept rubbing a fresh tattoo on his left arm. He saw me staring and pulled his sleeve down. *Whatever.*

We stopped and decided to make camp for the night. While Uncle Yo and I prepared dinner, Kisi and the healer prepared to treat Malcolm. The treatment wasn't comfortable. It was actually quite painful. The healer would have to find the source of his pain and bring it to the forefront of Malcolm's mind. He would then have to sit in the pain for a period, and once he had acknowledged it, then the healer could take the pain away, but the trauma would never be forgotten. I only knew because of what had happened to Uncle Yo.

A few years ago, Maame had gone off on a food run and had left us in Uncle Yo's care. We followed the rules and stayed quiet and hidden, but something found us anyway and all of us were kidnapped. They kept us in cages for the first few hours and came for Uncle Yo sometime after that.

We had never heard such screams come from Uncle Yo and he screamed the entire time they had him. When they returned him to his cage, he was in a horrific state. He was broken. We later found out that a monster had raped him. What added to the insidiousness, was that his power allowed for him to rape Uncle Yo's mind too.

When we were little, Maame had warned us about child molesters, but even she had little knowledge about *Blessed* who were child molesters. They didn't deserve to be a part of the *Blessed*. It was almost like giving monsters superpowers. They should have been called the Cursed—*Blessed* with amazing abilities and cursed to feel the need to use them for evil.

By the time Maame had tracked him down, it was too late. Uncle Yo was almost catatonic. He wouldn't talk, eat, or care for himself. Maame took him to five different healers, but none could heal him, because he wasn't *Blessed* and the pain was too deep.

A witch doctor from Argentina met up with us at a community, saying he could help. He said there was a procedure where he could transfer the pain to Maame. She would hold the pain for as long as she had to, then it would dissipate. It was dangerous and could leave a lasting effect, but Uncle Yo would not be in any more pain. Maame accepted.

The procedure took a full twenty-four hours and was the second most terrifying event in my life. Maame screamed in agony the entire time. The entire community gathered to try to help. When it was over, Uncle Yo seemed to be ok, but Maame disappeared for three days. No one knew where she went, but later, we heard that about thirty child predators had been mysteriously killed.

Kisi and the healer were ready for Malcolm. They laid him on a cot and required complete silence. Rodlin, Maame, and I waited outside a tiny tent. It seemed we had been waiting forever when we heard Malcolm cry out. "But she was my sister, my only sister!"

We heard a glass break and the healer called for all of us. We ran in and saw Malcolm struggling. He had been restrained, but had gotten his right wrist free. His eyes were still closed, and appeared to be putting up a fight from an unconscious state. Suddenly, he started to shed his human form and we all attempted to hold him down, but couldn't contain him. Transforming before us was a giant snake.

"Rodlin, now!" the healer screamed. I had been so busy trying to hold onto Malcolm, that I had barely noticed Rodlin getting bigger. His body was becoming larger than the tent and forming into a bubble of sorts, clear and enormous. He sucked Malcolm into his body, and Malcolm collapsed. After he had calmed down, Rodlin went to fetch water with Uncle Yo as Kisi and the healer finished the treatment.

Maame was angry that she hadn't been informed of Rodlin's *Blessed* status. "You could have put us all at risk, simply by withholding information!"

"I didn't tell you, because I didn't know enough. Nobody does. I have asked around, and no one has ever heard of his kind. I couldn't risk you not allowing us to travel with you, because of a lack of information. His power is terrifying."

Maame stopped pacing. "What do you mean terrifying?"

"The morning he found his parents, they were inside his clear bubble, dead. He couldn't remember anything after he woke up. He might have been protecting them from something, and they just... suffocated inside his bubble—I don't know!" Maame had a thoughtful look on her face. "Even if he was the one who killed them, it was undoubtedly an accident. A *Blessed's* first show of power is always most dangerous to those around them. That poor baby... we are never to speak of this unless he wants to, understand?" Kisi and I nodded. *So, Rodlin was Blessed?* Nonetheless, he still was as ugly as a boil in the summer heat.

* * *

We had finally made it to North Carolina. The boat was leaving from a place called Wilmington, and we still had a few days' journey ahead of us, so Maame was pushing us harder than ever. We had stopped too many times, and she was afraid we were running out of time. Much of North Carolina's coastal line had been broken off after The Great War as many creatures from the sea had risen during the battle. This part of our journey would be dangerous and tricky. Rodlin was clumsy and had almost fallen over three different cliffs. We needed to be careful. We had to walk close enough to the coast so we could see the boat, but far enough away so as not to fall in the water.

We walked for hours and decided to set up camp for the night. I actually wasn't tired and wanted to explore the area. North Carolina was beautiful and it was still light out. I asked Maame's permission to take a walk, and she said only if I brought someone with me. Of course, Rodlin volunteered, and suddenly, I wasn't in the mood for a walk anymore. I decided to check in with Malcolm as he was setting up his sleeping area.

"What do you want?" he asked with a scowl until he saw my facial expression. "I mean, can I help you?" He had been slightly nicer since his healing.

I plopped down beside him. "How do you feel?"

He stopped fidgeting with his cot and looked at me. "If you are trying to see if I'm going to still kill your mom, you can rest. I have no interest in hurting her, so it must have worked. It's weird, I still feel sadness, but not the pain that comes with it." Kisi was becoming a better healer by the day. *I wonder if she can take away the hatred I felt for our father?*

After dinner, I fell into a deep sleep. I dreamed that I was running in place and *Blessed* were chasing me, but no matter how hard I ran, I couldn't get away. Eventually, they all surrounded

125

me.

I woke up in a cold sweat. It was still nighttime; I could tell by the chirp of the insects. I had to go pee, but Kisi was laying across me. I gently pushed her off, and tip-toed out of our tent. After relieving myself, I headed back and was almost inside, when I heard voices coming from the trees behind me.

I quickly went to investigate and saw Maame speaking to someone I didn't recognize. "Don't make this bloody, Nanyamka. She needs to be with her kin. You will not be able to handle her when she transitions."

Maame scoffed. "You think your words hold weight? No. Not now, not ever. She is my daughter and I won't let her leave with relatives she does not know." They were speaking in English, but I couldn't catch everything.

"*Stepdaughter*. She is not your blood and she deserves to transition around her family!" I sat back. I knew Maame wasn't my birth mother. My mother had died when I was a baby and Maame married my father when I was two. Regardless, it still hurt to hear it from a stranger's lips. It still hurt to think about the fact that I did not come from Maame's womb. The stranger started walking towards my hiding place, but Maame didn't move. "I would be wise in your next decision. Shall I split you open, and then take out your assassin in the trees and the one behind the brush? Or are you going to be smart and walk away?"

The stranger turned his head in the moonlight, revealing his face. *He looks just like me! Who is he?* Maame stood up straight and got into her fighting stance as the man headed towards her. She was going to kill him.

I came out from behind the trees. "Wait! Please, Maame... don't kill them." The stranger stood where he was. There was an awkward silence that took place and sat on us all.

126

The stranger was the first to speak. "Mawusi, I am your Uncle Moon. Your mother's youngest sibling." While he talked, I studied his face. He had dark skin, long hair, and almond eyes. He looked just like me. "Did you hear the conversation we were having about you?" I nodded. "It's important for you to be around us when you transition. Normally, it wouldn't happen until you were an adult. But the stress of the End is making *Blessed* children transition sooner."

I walked closer to him. "Are you like me?"

He shook his head. "Not exactly." He took off his tunic. His skin started changing colors and his body stretched out. He grew wings and a tail. He looked like a mythical creature I had read about in a book when I was little, but I could not think of the name. He was terrifying. *Why can't I think of the name of this creature?*

The noise had woken Kisi up. "Aww cool, a dragon!" She came through the bushes and walked right up to the creature as it roared directly in her face. I camouflaged in preparation of killing it before it could harm her, but she just laughed and stroked its snout. The creature softened and blew smoke into Kisi's hand.

After Uncle Moon transformed back to his human form, we continued our conversation. "Based on your camouflaging abilities, we have suspicions of what you will become, but we are not completely sure." I listened to him go on about our family's history and it made my eyes heavy. I wanted to go back to sleep. I got up from where I was sitting and went and sat with Maame. I wrapped her arms around me and fell asleep, but I did not dream.

When I woke up in the morning, Maame was nowhere to be found. I panicked. *Did she leave me behind? Did she leave me with an Uncle I didn't know?* Frantically, I searched everywhere until

I spotted her on the beach, near the water, speaking to a water *Blessed*. Uncle Moon said good morning, but I was not ready to have that conversation.

I blew by him and ran to Maame. I gave her a big hug and started crying. "I thought you had left me."

Maame hugged me fiercely. "I would die before I left you. You are mine and I am yours. If you leave, it will be because we both felt it was best for your growth." I hugged her tighter and I didn't want to let go. She continued her conversation with the water Blessed. "So, you haven't seen the boat? It should have already been in the area, right?"

The water *Blessed* nodded. It resembled a squid mixed with human features. It had a beautiful short afro, that was still wet with sea water. *Simply gorgeous.* When it talked, the tentacles around its mouth moved. "Yes girl! We have been looking for that boat ourselves! It should have been passed through a week ago." I wasn't familiar with her accent. She spoke in English, but it was a different type of English.

I inquired to Maame about this and she chuckled. "It's African American Vernacular. Aunt ZaMia grew up in Oakland, California. Black folk from the Bay Area have an entirely different dialect of speak."

Aunt ZaMia seemed amused with the conversation. "Sis, yo' baby ain't never heard slang or hood shit before? Should I throw in a *'bee-yotch'* as well?" Maame and Aunt ZaMia erupted in giggles and I took it as my opportunity to escape any further ridicule.

I walked back to the camp. Uncle Moon had been waiting patiently for me near the top of the trail that led down to the beach, but I walked past him. I still wasn't ready. Instead, I went to find Malcolm, who was still asleep and snoring loudly. I nudged him gently, but he just grunted and farted. *Ewww.*

"Malcolm, wake up! I need your help."

Malcolm turned over. "Go away. Come back never!"

I rolled him back over to face me. "Malcolm, please. I need your help writing something in English, and I want to make sure I get my thoughts across."

It seemed to get his attention. Annoyed, he sat up and rubbed his eyes. "What could possibly be so important that you wake me when it's barely at sunrise?" Holding back tears, I told him about Uncle Moon, and how he wanted to take me, which seemed to soften his heart. "Do you even have a pen and paper?"

For the next thirty minutes, he helped me craft a letter to my uncle. I wanted to make sure it contained all my thoughts, and by the time we finished, it was time for breakfast. We walked back to the main group, where everyone was gathered in one place.

In English, I asked for everyone's attention, and when they were all quiet, I began my letter: "Dear Uncle Moon, I understand that you feel I would be better off with you and other family. I also understand that you fear for my welfare when I transition. You implied that Maame couldn't handle it. Let me tell you who Maame is. She is a warrior who slayed hundreds, if not thousands, of beasts with just a rake. She is a provider who puts everyone before herself. She has literally died so that our group can live. She is a problem solver. There has never been an issue that comes about, that she hasn't figured out. And finally, she is a nurturer, who does not stroke us with the same hands that have killed. You are free to travel with us as we head to Ghana, but I am not going anywhere with you if she is not there. She is mine and I am hers. And I want to make sure we all have an understanding." Uncle Moon had remained quiet the entire time I spoke. Once I finished, he nodded and stood up. "And also... if you ever dare diminish Maame's place in my life based off the fact that we are not blood-related, I will slit your throat." And with that, Uncle Moon headed back towards his group and was gone. Maame looked at me and attempted to hide her smile.

* * *

Within a day's travel, we had arrived at the area where the boat was supposed to be. There were several other groups there as well. Some groups I knew, but most I did not. The first day, we relaxed. We were all just happy to have arrived in time. The second day we went and gathered food for our group. The third day we started to get anxious and somewhat bored. By the time a full week had passed, Maame was worried and we began to bicker amongst ourselves.

She attempted to meet up with some of the relatives of those frozen in her tattoos. The war criminal's people never showed, so Maame removed him from her skin and left him frozen in the woods. Usually, she carefully aided in getting them unfrozen, but I suspected that she just wanted to be done with him, having fulfilled her obligation of getting him there. She still had my favorite flower on her face.

I decided to do nails to earn some extra cash. I met a group that was having a naming ceremony for a new baby. They all wanted their nails done and agreed to trade my services for jarred goods. I was meticulous with my craft. Sometimes, I used old bottles of nail polish I had picked up from random places, but most times, I made the polish myself, which gave the nails a henna effect. It was beautiful. I had done the entire ceremony party's nails and feet, and all but one person had paid up. I decided to wait until the day after the ceremony to talk to her.

I purposely greeted her in a respectful manner in which children greeted adults. "Auntie, your ceremonial gown was so beautiful. May I inquire when you will give me your payment of jarred goods for my service?"

The woman, who had been chatting with someone merrily, looked as if I had slapped her. "Wicked child! You dare come to me about payment? Your services were horrible." *Ouch.* "Leave before I slap the shit out of you in front of everyone!" *Double ouch.* I looked long and hard at her. I knew she would never put her hands on me, because she knew who my mother was. *But why this ridiculous display of power?* I was going to have to kill her.

A few years back, Maame had traded some goods to a man she didn't trust. We were low on food, and against her better judgment, she gave two of her weapons to a man who promised her jarred food. When it came time for him to uphold his end of the bargain, he was nowhere to be found. When she finally tracked him down, he was holed up in a brothel with members of his crew. We burst into his room where he was cuddled up with a *Blessed* creature that resembled a butterfly. After paying the creature for their service, Maame sent them off, and I could tell that things were going to be ugly. We assumed she wanted us to leave the room as well, but she told us to stay. She felt it was important for us to see what happened when people played with her money.

The man wasn't a reg. He was *Blessed* with the ability to grow one part of his body larger at a time. He knew he was going to be fighting Maame and his swelled left hand up to what seemed like the height of the ceiling. "Where are my jarred

131

goods, Lawrence?" The huge hand came crashing down slowly. Maame did a flip off the wall and landed on top of his huge hand, before running up his arm and kicking him in the head. For the next several minutes, she beat the crap out of him until he shakily pointed to a bag near the door. Inside was more than what he owed us for our weapons, but we took the entire bag as interest. As we were leaving, Maame spoke to the man in English. "I suggest you do better in your business practices, or next time swell your head up to anticipate getting your shit knocked off."

I thought about him as the woman turned her back on me. The disrespect of her dismissiveness hurt. Without thinking, I yanked her to the ground by her high bun. She screamed and attempted to grab me, but it was too late. I started beating her in the face and blood began to spill everywhere. A man attempted to grab me, but I knocked him down too. I sat on the woman's back and started to rip her nails off as she screamed in agony. I had just gotten to the second hand, when I felt myself being lifted off of her, and then everything went black.

When I awoke, Maame was sitting next to my cot. She was looking down and studying her hands. "Usi, do you know the things that I have done with these hands? I have killed so many with these hands. I have torn families apart with these hands. I have souls I will have to answer to in the afterlife, because of these hands. These hands have done so many heinous things."

I sat up and looked at them. Smooth, brown and lovely. "Maame, may I explain what happened?"

Maame shook her head. "I know exactly what happened. The healer checked your mind. I understand anger and pride. I also understand sometimes situations get out of control, but none of that happened today. Another reason why I fight first, is so that

132

you do not have to. You have me here. Your interaction with an adult, even a disrespectful one, should have been ran by me first and I would have handled it. You tore an entire hand of nails off that woman, Usi. If Rodlin hadn't bubbled you, you might have killed her. She was wrong, but it did not warrant her death or that level of pain." I felt bad. I hated when she was upset at me. "Forgive me for allowing you to think that this was ok." Maame left my tent and I laid down and cried myself to sleep. *What a horrible day.*

The next morning, I didn't want to leave my tent, but I knew I had to face the people. Maame wasn't one to hold grudges against her children, but I was still ashamed of myself.

I had barely folded up my tent when the woman approached me. Her hand was wrapped up in bandages, and her face was swollen and bruised. She looked terrified. "Here. I should have paid you when you completed the service. And when you came to me politely, I should have acknowledged you as a person. I am sorry."

I stood up and the woman flinched as I grabbed the jarred goods. "I apologize to you too, Auntie. Next time I will just get my Maame." The woman looked even more frightened at the mention of that and mumbled a goodbye, taking off quickly in another direction. I never saw her again.

* * *

The days waiting for the ship became weeks. Before we knew it, a month had gone by. Maame kept in constant communication with the *Blessed* from the water. No one had seen the boat. We were all becoming more worried every day. *Had we missed it? Were we in the wrong location? Where could it be?* Everyone tried their best to keep busy. We built a small community some distance from the shore and did our best to maintain.

After the incident, almost all the kids my age stayed away from me, which was fair since most of them were not killers. In addition, nobody wanted to get their nails done by me either. Soon, the heaviness came, a heaviness I wasn't used to. I probably could have gone to Kisi and the healer to ease the feeling, but I realized that I needed to feel it. *I needed to feel something.*

Before long, I got a babysitting gig watching Aunt ZaMia's children in the mornings. She always went hunting for fish and found it easier without the children. Her children had no human features at all. Each morning, I watched her squid babies swim in a shallow pool of water, surrounded by rocks on the beach. They were adorable, but quite mischievous. There was always one trying to climb out of the pool and play in the sand, which was starting to get on my nerves.

It had almost made it when I scooped it up. "Little one, please stay in the water." I kissed the baby gently on its head and placed it back in the pool, not realizing Aunt ZaMia was behind me.

"You have a very gentle presence, Usi." She extended four of her legs so that her babies could grab hold.

"Thank you, Auntie. See you tomorrow." She nodded and kissed me on the cheek. She had left a bag of fish by the rocks for me to give Maame. I picked the bag up, and it seemed exceptionally heavy today. I was still trying to figure out how to get the bag up the hill, when I heard someone scream. I froze in place to listen, and heard the scream again.

I ran faster than ever before, coming around the corner of some sharp rocks below a cliff. There, a kid was standing on a large rock screaming their head off. I stopped and the screaming continued. I looked around, but there didn't appear to be anyone hurting them. Maybe an invisible *Blessed*? They didn't appear to be in distress. *What's going on?*

The kid cupped their hands to scream again and I stopped them. "Are you ok?"

With dark brown almond shaped eyes, the kid lowered their hands. "Oy, I know you, mate. You're the kid that tore the nails off that lady thief! If you ask me, she deserved it! She had stolen from others before you." I recognized the accent. It sounded Australian.

I felt embarrassed, because of my English, so I wanted to make the conversation short. "It is not something I am proud of. Why are you screaming?"

The kid shrugged. "Don't know. Guess it just makes me feel better. The real question is, why did you come running? To save me?" I rolled my eyes and turned to leave. "Wait, don't go. I was just joking. My name is Martian, but my parents call me Mar."

I shook their hand. "My name is Mawusi, or Usi for short." I stared at their long hair, dark skin, soft facial features, and baggy clothes. "Are you a boy or a girl?"

Martian howled with laughter. "Neither, mate!" And just like that, I had made a friend.

From that point on, Martian and I were inseparable. We always met up in the morning after I finished babysitting and they were done screaming. Martian was interesting in every way. They had been in the United States for over five years, but still had a thick Aussie accent. They hated oatmeal and loved frogs. We caught and released frogs on a daily basis.

Martian's parents were especially interesting. They were what Maame called "a punk-rock, hot-ass mess!" They always wore all black, and often dressed in leather jackets. Both of them had ridiculous colored hair with multiple tattoos and face piercings. Martian's mom had deep brown skin with a huge afro. Martian's dad was brown as well, but looked a lot like Maame Siya in terms of facial features. They were amazing. They loved Martian and loved me by association. All three were *Blessed*.

Mar's mom was a virus. She could cause sickness in herself and spread it to others. As an adult, she learned to control it, but was still very dangerous. Mar's dad was an anti-virus—sort of like a healer, but more in the world of viruses. They met when they were both transitioning, and their abilities became infused. Now they were mates for life. Seeing them together made me happy. Their whole family seemed so content, and they were obsessed with Mar. They loved them so much. Watching them together reminded me of how things were when Maame Siya was with us. *Blissful*.

Martian's ability was they could predict the future a few minutes before certain events. Martian didn't like it, but I thought it was amazing! Once, I had almost tripped and sprained my ankle, and Mar caught me. "Mar, if you are this powerful at thirteen, think of how amazing you will be when we are adults!"

Mar shook their head and sighed. "Usi, when you have one parent that can bring death, and one parent that can bring life, being able to stop a sprained ankle hardly seems amazing." I hated when Mar talked like that. Their ability was so super cool, and one day, I knew it was going to save lives.

Later that evening, an elder called a meeting and asked for everyone in the community to attend. After dinner, we all settled on a spot close to the beach, so the water *Blessed* could attend. The elder who called the meeting was *Blessed* and could freeze time. I always liked this elder, but remained curious if they had ever stopped time around me. I settled near Kisi and Maame on a blanket. The elder stood completely still and waited for us all to settle down. He looked like a statue that was placed by the sea, so tall and noble.

When everyone had finally settled down, he spoke. "The boat is not coming." Everyone gasped. Maame who had been looking down at the baby while she was nursing, snapped her head up.

A man wearing nothing but a long skirt stood up. "What the hell do you mean, not coming? How do you know this? Where did you get your information from?" His comment sparked a frantic reaction amongst the crowd. Everyone started talking at once. Some started yelling while others broke out in prayer.

The elder remained patient and quiet until Maame shushed everyone. "I do not know where the boat is, or if it even ever existed," he said simply. "But I do know the safe haven in Ghana is real and we are going to have to find another way to get there. Right now, we are sitting ducks, and I alone don't have the conjure power to safeguard this community. We need to leave immediately."

After the meeting, we packed up our stuff to be ready for travel the following morning. We even packed our tents and had to lay down on the ground with just a blanket. I was sad. It felt like we had been chasing this boat forever, only to find out there wasn't one. It felt like betrayal.

I was so upset that not even Mar could cheer me up. "What if we split up? Your parents are so spontaneous. They might want to go a completely different direction than us!"

Mar chuckled. "This situation itself is spontaneous. Our lives are at the most spontaneous in all of spontaneity!" I fell out laughing. Mar always found a way to make me laugh.

"Ok. Can I at least give you my Maame Siya's summoning

name? That way you can summon her and find me."

Mar nodded. "Actually, my parents are about to call me to come pack up my stuff. I will be right back!" I waited for Mar to return, but after two hours, I figured they had gotten busy packing and fell asleep. I guess I would have to catch them in the morning. I was sleepy anyway.

* * *

"Usi, Usi! You have to wake up now!" I was in a good sleep and couldn't understand why Mar was shaking me. They were breathing heavily, as if they had sprinted the entire way over. "Usi, you have to wake up and warn your family. Something horrible is about to happen."

I jumped up. Based on our experiments with Mar's powers, I had less than five minutes before something bad happened. I quickly woke Maame and the rest of our camp. Everyone got up quickly to grab their things. Having already packed, made for an easy exit. Maame gave the baby to Uncle Yo, and we all started running towards the larger camp. I looked at my watch. We had one minute and forty seconds max.

Maame yelled to the other campers. "Get up! Get up now!" A few people peeked out their tents, but nobody moved. We all started screaming for people to wake up. Slowly, people started waking up and pushing their blankets back. Mar hadn't gotten a chance to tell me what was going to happen, so we had no answer for the people who were inquiring. I looked at my watch. Thirty seconds.

"Nanyamka!" Someone was calling out for Maame, and suddenly, a person came running out of the forest wearing all black. I squinted in the dark. *Uncle Hiroji?* This couldn't be good.

He was supposed to be in Ghana already. *Why do I feel like we're in deep shit?* Whatever was coming was big! Uncle Hiroji screamed to Maame again. "Nanyamka, run!"

V

Part Five

"I can't promise that things will get better. I can only assure you that things change. Hopefully within that change you find peace."

LaKiera Jones (Pre-apocalypse)

Her skin was peeling more than usual. Watching her try different body washes, lotions, and cremes was exhausting. These were things I never had to worry about with my blue skin. We were absolutely forbidden from intervening with the *Blessed*. The rules for members of the Radar were strict, and we were not shown any mercy just because of our positions. If caught intervening, we would assuredly die a painfully horrendous death. Our role was to watch over them, and make sure they did not violate any rules and regulations. Still, it would be most fulfilling if I could tell her that she was transitioning.

* * *

Life sucked so bad right now. Today was probably going to be my second write up, and my eczema was exceptionally crappy. I'm the lizard lady today. Rubbing cream on my face wasn't helping; in fact, it seemed like it was making things worse. Three more stop lights, and I would be at work. Just three. I looked in the driver's side mirror. My eyes looked sad. How else should a college graduate rushing to a job that only required a high school diploma look? The bills needed to be paid and being a manager at a call center helped. I glanced down at my phone and saw Amina had texted. It was her dad's week, and she had forgotten her soccer gear at home. A second text came in. And edge control? This girl was 11, why does she need her edges laid all the time? Damn it. I wonder did Dom still have a key to my place? I would contact him when I got to work.

I knew my supervisor was going to be on my ass for being five minutes late. It didn't help that I looked like a lizard with colorful braids in my hair. I rushed inside and saw his back was turned as he chastised one of my coworkers, which gave me an opportunity to slip in. I had barely turned on my computer and slipped on my headset when I felt him behind me. He always did this creepy thing where he stood behind people to spy on what they were doing. He thought because we had our headsets on, we wouldn't be able to hear him, but we always knew he was there. *Always.*

After about a minute, he tapped me on the shoulder and called my name. I turned around. "Oh, hi Mr. Flamscans. How are you doing?" Looking sternly over his glasses, he attempted to finger-wag me about my tardiness. Almost on cue, my phone rang. Putting up my finger to interrupt him, I jumped into my customer service role. After about thirty seconds, he found another victim. I looked five cubicles to the left and folded my hands in prayer as a thank you to my coworker Marina. We had come up with a system where we called one another if Flamscans came to our desk, and it always worked, because he took his job way too seriously. Marina winked and gave me the thumbs up.

* * *

Thankfully, Dom still had a key to my house and didn't mind

grabbing Amina's things. We did so well with our daughter. We each had her one week and brought her back on Sunday. We respected each other's boundaries, never fought about money, and put Amina's needs before our own. I couldn't have chosen a better person to coparent with. The best part of all, was that Amina genuinely seemed happy and content.

I was only five hours into my ridiculous shift, when I felt a burning itch across my neck. I attempted to rub the itch away gently, when a huge piece of skin from back of my neck flaked off into my hands . *What the—!*

"LaKiera?" Mr. Flamscans had actually managed to sneak up on me. *Good for him, but this was a bad time.* Something was going on with me, and I needed to find out what. I hadn't taken my lunch, and this appeared to be the perfect opportunity.

As Flamscans talked to me about keeping the crew in line and work merit, I gathered my things and headed to the elevator, but the goof followed me all the way there. "I think you make some really good points, sir. I would love to discuss them more when I get back from lunch." He continued to talk even after the elevator doors had closed.

I had to stop myself from sprinting to the car. In the elevator, a piece of skin from my arm came off. It was like I was shedding. Closing my car door, I tried to catch my breath. *What should I do? Hospital? Home?* I glanced at the time. I knew it would be high traffic on the roads. *Shit.* Maybe I could just find an empty parking lot to collect my thoughts. I headed away from my work, itching all over. I was terrified to scratch myself. I was starting to feel like my entire body was on fire. If I didn't scratch, I was going to crash. A stop light was coming up. Good. Slowing to a stop, I scratched feverishly. Skin started coming off from everywhere. My face, my arms, my scalp. My freshly braided box-braids were no more. I had scratched my entire scalp off. Luckily, the light was incredibly long. I looked over and saw two terrified faces pressed up to the glass in the car next to me. I tried to smile at them, but they just screamed. I needed to get away from people. *Why couldn't I find that empty parking lot?* I could only imagine what I looked like.

After driving a few miles, I came to a river access point that had a few parking spaces. There was only one other car there, and their windows were fogged up and steamy. I doubted they would even notice me. Nervously, I pulled my mirror down in my car to see what I looked like and screamed.

I was different. My milky brown skin was gone and was now a smooth, rich mahogany. My tight curls were no more and in their place were loose, dark black ringlets. My lips were bigger and my light brown eyes were darker. It was weird. I looked like a completely different version of myself. I screamed again and jumped out of the car.

No, no, no. This can't be happening! How did I shed into a new person? Something had to be wrong with me. Maybe I had a virus—a flesh-eating, rapid hair growth, eye-color-changing virus. I had to go to the hospital. I reached to open the car door, when somebody closed it. I looked up and saw the strangest thing standing in front of me, blocking me from entering my car. I screamed and passed out.

* * *

Opening my eyes slowly, I saw that the thing was still there. I sat up from the ground to study it. It appeared to be naked, but there were no private areas visible. It was dark blue, and completely hairless all over. It had no face, but darker blue spots where its eyes, nose, and mouth should be. It had to be about eight feet tall, and I should have been more terrified, but I wasn't scared anymore. It actually had a calming presence.

"Forgive my voice. This is the first time I have ever used it. I know you want to rush to the hospital, but they wouldn't understand what you are going through." I wasn't sure if it was some freak in a suit, but the tears I had been holding back began to fall. I fumbled in my purse for my compact and some tissue, but made sure to keep my eyes on the being. "It's called a transition. Many languages have a word for what they are. You have mostly Ghanaian in your bloodline, so you might use the word 'abosomakoter' or 'chameleon.' You shed your skin as a part of blending in for survival purposes. In most cases, you would be surrounded by others who are *Blessed* and this wouldn't be so shocking. But you have been disconnected due to the interruption in your history." Suddenly, it had my full attention. "Most people have others around them who have transitioned into the *Blessed* version of themselves. A grandma, an aunt or an older relative is usually around to help them through the transition. Though you have family, none of them can help you, because so far you are the only person in your current line who is *Blessed*."

I needed to sit down. I opened my car door and sat with my legs hanging out of the car. I had a trillion questions. "Why am I transitioning? When will it stop?"

The area where the being's face should have been held a lot of expressions. The darker blue spots seemed to move with its voice and it flashed something that looked like it was trying to smile. "That is the beauty of it all—nobody knows. You transition how you transition. I have to go now. I could die for this encounter. Just know that I am your keeper and I am always watching."

This is way too much. But I knew I couldn't just let it leave. "Wait, what do I do from here? What do I tell my family? My job? You know, the people that *know* what I look like? I cannot just show up with this hair and this skin..." I glanced at my eyes in the compact, which had turned a dark green. "These eyes! I need help!"

I was terrified and the being knew it. "There is a woman that runs an orthopedic shop off 8th and L. Go see her tomorrow." I was barely able to write down the intersection before I looked up and saw that I was alone. *Ok, this is about to get ridiculous.*

* * *

Sleeping was out of the question. I was still shedding. My nails, eyelashes and teeth had come out all over my apartment. I had even shed a few pounds. *What am I going to tell Amina? Will she even recognize me?* Since I couldn't sleep, I spent hours online trying to figure out more of what was going on with me. By the time I looked up at the clock, it was 3 am. I closed my eyes and dreamed.

I was a chameleon. And not a cute one that hangs out on a tree in the tropics, but a huge monstrous one. I could blend into any background and hunt people down. I was a monster.

I awoke in a cold sweat. I looked at the clock. 3 PM? *You have to be kidding me... I slept for twelve hours?!* I glanced at my phone and saw my job had called three times. I called the assistant manager and explained that I was sick and decided to get a doctor's note before heading to the orthopedic shop.

Thankfully, urgent care was fairly empty. After checking in with the receptionist, I checked in with Dom, thinking that I might need him to keep Amina during my week. I knew he was

148

off today, so I took a breath and videocalled him. He answered on the third ring.

Before I could say anything, he commented on my appearance. "What happened to your face? Are you at the hospital? What's wrong?" I hated that he knew me so well. Tears started to fill my eyes. "Send me your location, I'm on my way."

We had the weirdest relationship. We were horrible lovers, but amazing friends and extraordinary co-parents. We acknowledged this shortly after getting pregnant with Amina and decided not to force something that wasn't there.

About thirty minutes later, Dom rushed in. As soon as I saw him, I burst into tears and told him everything.

"So, you shed your entire body... like a snake?"

"Snakes aren't the only reptiles that shed."

Dom shook his head. "That's neither here nor there, Ke. You look like an entirely different person. This has to be a disease... or a virus or... *something!* There has to be an explanation! What the hell are we going to tell Mina?"

I couldn't stop crying. "I don't know! I just need to get this sick note for my job, so I can hurry downtown to see that lady. Her shop closes soon."

Dom got really quiet. "So, some blue alien-thing came out of nowhere and gave you an address to some mysterious-ass place to get help? I'm going with you. I'll call my mom and have her pick up Mina from the after school program. We are figuring this out together."

No sooner had Dom hung up with his mother, I was called to the back and we made our way to the vitals station. The nurse slid the cuff around my arm to get my blood pressure and waited. "That's odd, either you're dead or you have the lowest pulse I have ever seen." Dom and I glanced nervously at each other. The nurse tried several more times and could only manage to get a faint reading. She decided to move on, but every test seemed to fail. She couldn't hear my heart, test my reflexes or even draw blood as the needle kept breaking off against my skin. After a frustrating thirty minutes, she decided to go get the doctor.

"Dom, look at the time. The shop closes in twenty-five minutes. If we don't leave now, we will never make it."

He frowned. "Ok, but if we leave now, you won't get your note... or the opinion of an actual doctor." He had a good point, but I felt that seeing the woman was much more urgent.

We hadn't yet made up our minds when the doctor burst in. He seemed flustered and out of breath. "Hi. Mrs. Jones. My name is Dr. Perry. I just spoke to the nurse and she said there were some complications with your vitals. I would be happy to help." As we watched him put on his gloves, there was something eerie about him. In fact, there had been something eerie about the entire encounter. Dom must have felt it too as we began to study him closely.

"I'm sorry, our daughter's school called right before you came in," Dom said. "We are going to have to come back."

A flash of anger came over the doctor's face, and just as quickly, a look of forced calm washed over him. "Are-are you sure? It won't take long. I have completed exams in as little as five minutes. It'll be really quick." He was making me uncomfortable.

"Thank you, but our daughter comes first," Dom said as we stood up and damn near ran out of the building. We got into our cars and headed to the orthopedic shop.

The open sign had just turned off when we pulled up. I jumped out the car as Dom was still parking his car and ran up to the door, but it was already locked. I knocked gently against the glass. "Hello. I need to talk to someone. Please, if you are in there, I would really like to talk." Dom had finally finished parking and walked up to the door to knock with me, but nobody came. I could tell that they had just turned off the sign, so they couldn't be far. "Please... if you are in there, I need to talk. I was told you could help me with my shedding skin." Within seconds, a face appeared in front of the glass. *Where the hell did she come from?* A tiny woman pointed and mouthed for us to meet her around back. The back of the building was creepy, which went with the theme of the day. I was glad Dom was with me.

The older woman opened the door and motioned for us to come in. The door had barely closed when she pulled out a machete. "If you two are here to rob me, I'll cut your head off!" Shaking, I put my hands up and assured her that we meant no harm. "What do you want? Start from the beginning."

We all sat down slowly and I told her everything. I pulled out my phone to show her a picture from when I'd recently gotten my hair braided. "This is what I looked like yesterday morning. And now I look like this."

The woman had been mostly quiet up until then. "This being who told you to contact me... you said it was dark blue with no hair?" I nodded. The woman sighed. "Well, you are in the right place, but what I am going to show you is well beyond your realm of thinking as a human. Are you sure you're ready?"

Dom squeezed my hand. I wasn't prepared for shit, but I was already there. "Yes."

The woman closed all the curtains in her shop, then took off her clothes. *This is what I get for believing some creep in a skin-tight blue suit. This old lady is about to strip for us.* As the woman stood in front of us completely naked, all I could think of was the amount of apology cookies I would have to bake for Dom. I glanced over to see how he was taking in the experience when he gently turned my head back towards the woman. Something was happening.

Her brown skin was turning colors. A rich, dark purple and then a greenish-blue. Her body started shedding. Her limbs were changing and she went down on all fours. It was both frightening and amazing. Her body continued to shed and morph until standing before us was a giant a chameleon. She climbed up the wall and stuck out her freakishly long tongue at us. *Show off.*

It took about six minutes for the woman to transform back into her human form. We helped her put on her clothes and found a bottle of water for her to drink. She seemed exhausted. "I used to be able to transform so effortlessly, but now I am getting old." I had so many questions, but I was at a loss of words. Seeing my facial expression, she sank back into her seat. "Let's start from the beginning. You are a chameleon. I don't know what the name in your tribe would be—it varies depending on your lineage. I am from a tribe called the Enawene Nawe, an indigenous people from Brazil. When I transitioned, my family had a huge ceremony for all of us who were *Blessed.*"

Over the next few hours, she attempted to pass down a lifetime's worth of knowledge. From what I could tell, there were metahumans who could blend in and other creatures who could not. I was a part of a group called *Blessed.*

I stood up and started doing jumping jacks. The older woman looked at me, and then Dom, for an explanation. "Don't worry... she used to have really bad anxiety as a kid and her middle school counselor told her to do jumping jacks to help. It's supposed to increase her heart rate and lower the anxiety in her stomach. She does it sometimes to bring herself back down." The woman must have found Dom's explanation satisfactory. She sat back, closed her eyes and waited for me to finish.

After ninety or so, I finally collapsed, but it had barely helped. The room still felt too small and my anxiety was still through the roof. "Will I ever look like myself again?"

The woman stifled a chuckle when she saw how serious I was. "Follow me." We followed her through a door and up a set of stairs into some sort of living space. She led us to a small altar with pictures all over it. She lit three candles and waited. I took my time looking at all the pictures. All the women were beautiful.

"Are these your relatives who have passed on?"

She smiled. "No child, these are all pictures of me." I almost fainted. There were at least twenty pictures on the altar. Some appeared to be really old from the 1800s and a few were photographs of men.

I sat down on the floor. Dom attempted to sit down beside me to console me, but the woman stopped him. "No, this is her journey alone."

* * *

I laid on her floor and fell asleep. While I slept, I had vivid dreams of changing into a different person every day. I awoke in a cold sweat, but I was no longer in the living room with the altar. I was in a small room with a single candle and I could hear voices outside the door. I could hear Dom and the older woman speaking. The door was halfway open with just enough space to squeeze through. I didn't really want to face anyone, but I knew I had to.

I peeked around the corner and saw the woman wiping the counter in the kitchen, while Dom sat on the couch, sipping from a cup. I came into his full view, but he never turned his head.

The woman looked directly at me. "Were you never taught that it's rude to spy on others?" *Spy?* Dom seemed confused. He looked past me and asked the woman who she was talking to. She chuckled. "Do you even realize that you are camouflaged right now? I have had this skill since I was eleven." I looked down at where my body was supposed to be and saw the floor and the carpet in a blur. "Sit down child, I have much more to pass down."

Dom and I didn't leave until after 4 AM. She told me that I would be able to camouflage and could even turn full chameleon, and also that I would transform into another version of myself every few years. My mind was all over the place and I needed to sleep. I was exhausted and wanted to go home, but left my car in front of the woman's place since we were closer to Dom's house and he didn't trust me to drive.

We pulled up to Dom's apartments and I felt my shoulders finally relax. I was probably going to sleep for another twelve hours. It was still dark out, but the streetlights were on. Dom rubbed his eyes. "Today has been an adventure. We both can use some rest. I'll take Mina's room." I loved him for many reasons, but especially for tonight: he had been my savior. I would never have been able to process this situation without him.

I reached down into my purse when something caught my eye across the parking lot. It looked like two men were walking by Dom's apartment building, but it was how they were walking that caught my attention. Dom went to open his door, but I stopped him for fear that they might see the lights come on inside his car.

I pointed to the men and Dom squinted his eyes before attempting to shrug them off. "But look at how they are walking... It's so weird and out of place. Don't you remember the woman saying there are all types of creatures in the *Blessed* world? What if those are some of the other creatures?"

Dom yawned. "Ke, we are both exhausted. All I see are two men who probably had too many. They're just a couple of guys who..." He stopped short and his eyes grew wide. "...are SCALING THE WALL OUTSIDE MY BUILDING!" I quickly put my hand over his mouth to keep him from screaming. The men crawled up the wall like spiders. One of them had a long trench coat that looked strangely familiar. *Where have I seen that coat?* I needed a better look.

I reached for the door handle and Dom grabbed me. "Are you out of your mind? We don't know what those things are or why they are crawling around my apartment, but I have to assume they aren't here for a good reasons." I went to grab the handle again. "LaKiera Ann Jones, I forbid you from leaving this car!"

I gave him a look and grabbed his face, kissing him on the cheek. "Felipe Dominic Washington, I need you to trust me. Plus, I'm pretty sure I just figured out how to camouflage."

I tested out my theory and he looked around frantically. "Ke? Ke! Are you camouflaging now or did you leave?" I was still standing in the same space, but I didn't want to be seen. It was just that simple: if I thought about it, then it happened instantly.

I slipped away from the car and approached the building slowly. My eyesight was perfect in the dark, so I crept to an area with less light, so I could watch as they continued to climb the wall. As I got closer, I got a bad feeling in the pit of my stomach. Whatever was about to happen was not going to be good. It wasn't too late to turn around and get back in the car with Dom. I thought about running back to safety, but I was too scared to look at him.

As they continued their climb, I glanced at the men and froze in my spot. One of them was definitely familiar. I had to get closer. I recognized the coat, but it was his voice that gave him away. *Mr. Flamscans? He was a part of the Blessed? Now might be a good time for some jumping jacks.* I started to ponder how many other people I knew that could be walking amongst us as superhumans. The better question was why Flamscans was outside Dom's building at four in the morning.

I finally got closer and attempted to listen to what they were saying, but they were speaking in a language I had never heard. It sounded like a series of clicks and hisses and sent chills through my body. Suddenly, they switched to English and I could tell the other man was upset at Flamscans, but I couldn't figure out why. I moved in closer, standing directly under the other man. I realized he was the weird doctor from the urgent care clinic. This couldn't be a coincidence. *How did he and Mr. Flamscans know where Dom lived?* Then it hit me that Dom was my emergency contact for just about everything and his information was on my file at work.

Without realizing it, I started to scale the wall so I could listen in on their conversation. When I was just a few feet off the ground, I grew scared and fell into a nearby bush. I froze and waited, hoping they hadn't noticed.

"You might as well come out—we all know you haven't mastered your abilities yet. Let's not waste time."

I was annoyed by the dryness in Flamscans' voice attempting to lure me out. I considered myself a movie connoisseur. In every film where the villain attempted to lure someone out under the false promises of safety or a swift death, the person was usually met with something far worse. *Does he think I'm Boo-Boo The Fool?* I concentrated on camouflaging. Before I left the bushes,

I had to make sure they couldn't see me.

I peeked my head out the bushes and almost passed out. The doctor and Flamscans were gone, and in their place were two toddler-sized spiders. I froze as they hissed at each other, but neither pounced on me. I must have still been camouflaged. I slipped out the bushes and attempted to scale the walls again, but it didn't work. I was concentrating too hard and the old woman had assured me that my abilities were supposed to come effortlessly, that they should be as natural as breathing. *So why couldn't I scale this damn wall?*

The sound of me scuffling around on the wall caught the attention of one of the spiders and it quietly began to make its way towards me as the other followed closely behind. I froze, frightened that my camouflage wouldn't work. I had one foot on the wall while the other was still placed firmly against the ground and refused to move for fear they might notice. The spiders remained frozen in place as well. We were having a good ol' fashioned "freeze-off" and I intended to win. I stood there for several moments until they felt satisfied I wasn't in the area. They turned to check other parts of the wall, assuming I had climbed up. I needed a different approach to get near them.

I moved away from the bushes and attempted to scale a different section of the wall. I went to lift up my leg, but my arm was snagged on something I couldn't see. The more I pulled, the tighter it became. I realized they'd planted a web trap and my goofy ass had walked right into it. *Shit.*

I was so busy trying to unhook myself, I barely noticed one of the spiders descending upon me. It hissed to the other spider, which came over quickly. With one of its long legs, the spider felt around for its line of web and pulled me towards it. I tried to remember if there was something the older woman had said that might help, but nothing came to mind and I began to panic. I was just inches away from the spider and had no idea what to do.

Suddenly, something she had said popped in my mind. "Your body will know what to do—you just have to trust it and trust yourself." *What could it mean?*

The spider had me in its grasp and began to spin me around in a cocoon. Before I knew what was happening, my tongue was out and the spider hissed. I wrapped my long, thick tongue around the spider's head and it screamed. *A loud, human-like scream.*

I looked down and saw that my body had started to transform. My human shape shed away to the sidewalk and my chameleon form took over as my eyes shifted to the side of my head. I broke free from the web that had me halfway bound and landed on all fours. My brown skin had turned a deep bluish-green and felt rough all over. I barely felt the other spider biting me, attempting to force me to free its friend.

My mind was still mine, but I felt completely different. My eyes seemed to be directly connected to my stomach and I was hungry. In one swift motion, I swallowed the spider that I had been holding on to. It tasted delicious.

Within moments, the other spider transformed back into its naked human state. Flamscans put his hands up and through his groveling at my feet, I realized why they were looking for me—I was a predator, *their* predator. They were hoping my fresh transition would be an opportunity to pounce on my naivety.

I scoffed and turned my head back to Dom, still in my chameleon form. Flamscans was still trying to come to some sort of resolve behind me, because he didn't feel safe. "So, about that raise you asked for two years ago..." he said with a nervous smile. I looked back at him, and with my chameleon hands, tried my best to flip him off.

Nanyamka

"**N**anyamka, run!" Hiroji yelled. I could barely make him out in the dark. All I saw were shadows coming from the trees. Whatever he was running from must have been terrifying because Hiroji was no punk. This didn't make sense—he was supposed to be in Ghana already.

I couldn't see in the dark, but I could hear something. *Something big.* Hiroji was still calling me, but the confusion was too much. I looked around for the kids. Suddenly, Siya appeared and grabbed Kisi before disappearing into another dimension.

She came back quickly to grab Yokow as Hiroji finally caught up to my side. "Nany, we have to get out of here. This is serious." I couldn't see his facial expressions, but I could tell he was completely out of breath.

"Where can we go, Hiro? We are backed against a cliff. Should we jump into the water? What's chasing you?" Before he could reply, ZaMia rose from the water in her *Blessed* form. She was a deity, an orisha named Yemoja. Rising up from the water in her full form, she was over a hundred feet tall! With glowing eyes and several octopus-like arms, she swooped half the group into her arms before sliding back down into the water. I saw that she had grabbed Usi and her friend Mar as well and knew they would be safe. Everyone else disappeared with those who could travel through space and time. The only ones left on the cliff were Hiroji, the baby and me.

* * *

When we were twelve, Hiroji convinced me to fight a vampire. It was a legacy vamp, meaning both its parents had been vampires as well. Legacy vamps were dangerous because they were incredibly strong, unlike halfies, or those who had gotten bitten and turned. We grew up near a lowkey vamp club for teens on the east side. Hiroji was *Blessed* and could get us into any dark and scary place. A lot of us went there to fight and rebel against our parents.

This particular club had a cage in the back for fighting. After dancing and partaking in party favors, Hiroji pressured me to challenge a vamp that looked my age. I was terrified. I had fought both regs and *Blessed* alike, but it had always been under the watchful eye of my father. In the back of my mind, I knew I was still safe if anything went south. But here, I was in a room full of vamps who were known for breaking rules. My only advantage was that my opponent couldn't have been older than fifty, an infant in vamp years. I was praying he lacked experience.

The bell had barely rung for us to start when the vamp charged at me. His face had already started transforming and I knew I had little time before he was at full strength. I dodged him easily and saw an opening to break his jaw, but I didn't act fast enough. I went to throw the punch and he blocked me. Smiling, he stood up straight. Just that quickly, he had grown over three inches and popped out his teeth, revealing two shiny fangs. *Damn.*

He grabbed my arm and threw me across the cage. The impact

damn near knocked me out. I struggled to stand as he strolled to my side. He was hungry and could smell my blood through my flesh. His eyes turned black and his voice grew deeper. "Should I eat you now or later? Father says I need to start accumulating pretty items for my collection and you would add to it perfectly."

I surprised him with a headbutt and he stumbled into the side of the cage. I charged forward and uppercut his left jaw. Vamp anatomy was different than regs, so each blow needed to count. I started throwing calculated jabs to his rib cage, but he simply stood up straight, unscathed. *I didn't even make a dent!*

"Enough!" he let out, grabbing me by the neck and pushing me against the cage. He revealed his hideously grey tongue, sliding its full length across my cheek. I kept clawing at his hands around my neck, but he was too strong. "I could turn you right now. A quick bite to the neck and you'll be mine forever." He slid his hands between my legs and sniffed the air. "I can smell your menstrual coming soon. Good—that means you're ready to have my child." *Why do they always have to become creepy predators once they transform?*

I felt helpless. I knew Hiroji was somewhere in the crowd, but he was forbidden to jump into a one-on-one. I was starting to get dizzy and estimated I had about two minutes left before I passed out. If I did, I would be his forever. I had to think fast. I punched and kicked, and even tried pinching him, but nothing was working.

He had a death grip around my neck and I felt myself getting tired from struggling. "Stop fighting me!" he snarled before a smile crept across his lips. "Actually, I like my girls with a little fight in them."

Suddenly, I snapped. Without thinking, I did half the blue-ring octopus, a pressure point technique that would cause death if all eight points were activated. He went limp and fell to the floor as the room went quiet. The four points I had activated would only provide a temporary paralysis. I started to exit the ring when a large vamp hopped over the caged fence, landing hard on the mat. He wanted to challenge me, but I shook my head and continued towards the exit.

Another vamp blocked the way. "Either fight or die, reg!" he sneered. I was exhausted and my back was hurting from where I had been thrown into the fence. I didn't want to fight, but I sure as hell didn't want to die. The two vamps were beginning to close in on me. I kept backing up until I was all the way against the cage fence. *Where the hell was Hiroji?* I got into my fighting stance and the bigger vamp lunged at me. I dodged him, but it put me closer to the smaller vamp whose eyes had already turned black. He grabbed me and I tried to break away, but his grip was ridiculously tight. The bigger one closed in. *This is it. This is how I die.*

I closed my eyes, and suddenly, there was a loud thump against the mat. Hiroji had finally decided to make an entrance. He was part of a unique group of *Blessed* that originated in Japan called the *Shussei māku irezumi*, which he referred to as "Zumis." They were all born with a birthmark that resembled a tattoo, which they could grab from their skin and materialize into real weapons. Hiroji was born with two swords across his back. Although he was only thirteen, he had been allowed to get six additional tattoos. His family wanted him to be able to train his gift with different weapons. Most recently, he had been honing his skills with the dragon down his side. The vamps looked terrified. There was not a lot of information about Hiroji's kind as they had existed in the shadows for centuries. Living amongst regs, they only used their abilities when absolutely necessary, so the vamps had little knowledge on how to fight him.

"This reg is under my protection," he said calmly. "I'm going to allow you to honor the rule of the cage and let her out, considering she disabled your friend over there." Hiroji had little patience, and as proof of his gangsta, he pulled the snake tattoo from his left arm, transforming it into a large python right before our eyes. It was both frightening and amazing. The vamps backed into the cage fence. Hiroji looked at the vamps and then at the python before giving me a smile. "Want to see whose fangs are bigger?"

* * *

Siya popped back, exhausted. She had never successfully transported other people and did not look well. "Come on," she said to me.

I shook my head. "Take Hiroji instead." They both started to yell in protest, but we didn't have time. I pushed them both off the cliff and Siya transported them in mid-air. *Good. Now it was time.*

As I stood there on the cliff, my father's words seemed ever pertinent. I made sure the baby was wrapped tightly on my back and got into my stance. Now I just needed to know what the hell I was fighting. I still could not see what was coming from the forest, but I could feel it.

I was familiar with danger. It was ever present in all aspects of my life. From the moment I woke up in the morning to the time my children fell back asleep at night, I remained on alert. This heightened sense of awareness was what had kept us alive for so long and I wasn't ready to die yet. I had shit to do.

* * *

When I was three, my father had told me that fighting was a matter of physics. If I used kinematic equations, I would have the ability to beat my opponent every time. He broke it down as best he could to a three-year-old and I absorbed every bit of it into my toddler brain. "Nany, you will only have a matter of seconds to figure out how much force needs to be distributed to your opponent. You will need to determine the energy that needs to be put forth in one swift motion. Their weight and height need to be calculated, so you can distribute the force properly, all while being aware of your own velocity."

Then, he told me to knock him down. At the time, I had only been training for a year and could barely knock Hiroji down, much less my own father. Based on what he taught me, I tried my best, but still failed everyday. It seemed to be a near impossible task, because there was a drastic difference between our height and weight. I voiced my concerns to him and he went completely quiet.

After some time, he finally spoke. "Nany, what is waiting for you outside these walls comes in all shapes and sizes. What I am preparing you for is beyond your comprehension, but I cannot leave this earth until I know that you can survive. Think of your opponent as matter. You're simply shifting matter in space and time."

About the Author

Chi Chavanu Àse is a Science Fiction/Fantasy author who was first introduced to Sci-fi by her mother at an early age. Often sent to her room for misbehaving, she would curl up in a blanket with one of her mother's books which subsequently ignited the spark that would fuel her love for literature. She initially began writing and performing poetry at the age of twelve. Over time, she began to notice how difficult it was to find books that she could associate or identify with the characters, given the lack of representation. Thus, it became her greatest desire that little Black children would see themselves represented in every genre, especially sci-fi. Her first book, *Journey to Ghana and Other Stories*, focuses entirely on the Black experience. Likewise, it is her desire to continue writing stories and producing literary work that Black people can see themselves represented in. Chi currently resides in California with her fine-ass husband and amazing children.

Made in the USA
Coppell, TX
26 July 2023